MW00618137

The Elven Star

BIANCA D'ARC

HAWK PUBLISHING, LLC

Copyright © 2023 by Bianca D'Arc

All rights reserved.

No part of this publication may be reproduced, distributed, or transmitted in any form or by any means, including photocopying, recording, or other electronic or mechanical methods, without the prior written permission of the author, except as permitted by U.S. copyright law.

The story, all names, characters, and incidents portrayed in this production are fictitious. No identification with actual persons (living or deceased), places, buildings, and products is intended or should be inferred.

To Mom and Dad.

I miss you.

Prologue

The dryad Leonora had been stuck inside a willow tree for a very long time. She'd asked to be put within by choice. It had really been the only thing to do after she'd been shot by a poisonous silver bullet. Her old friend, the vampire Master Dmitri, had given her a few drops of his immortal blood in order to stave off the poison, but she knew the amount of magic—and the particular kind of magic—needed to save her life would be hard to gather.

She had asked her newly discovered many-times-great-granddaughter to find the others like her. The descendants of Leonora's daughter, Marisol, who had been lost down through the generations. Those women, together, might have a chance at restoring Leonora to the land of the living. If nothing else, it would be a good exercise for Sally, the former police detective who had just mated with the local wolf Alpha.

Leonora's cottage was within the wolf Pack's territory, and she had long had a good relationship with them. She liked werewolves. She especially liked to watch the little ones play and frolic through the forest. They were such happy creatures, and they took good care of the land they lived on, which meant so much to Leonora.

She'd been hanging out in the willow tree, suspended between life and death, the mortal realm and another place where time didn't matter quite so much. She tried not to worry too much. She tried to just drift a bit and let Fate do as

She willed. Leonora trusted in the Mother of All to do whatever was the right thing regarding her own continued existence. If she was meant to live on, Sally would be successful in finding her long-lost kin. If not, well, Leonora had been alive a very long time, and perhaps it was time to move on to the next realm.

She wasn't really sure where earth elementals like herself would move on to when their time was done in the mortal realm, but she wasn't afraid of it. She would miss her friends, though. Leonora was aware of them, sometimes, visiting her resting place.

She was aware of Dmitri, keeping his promise to help protect her resting place. He would come at night, sometimes with his mate, sometimes on his own. Sally visited too. And she brought other women, as she found them. Leonora was really impressed by how many of her descendants Sally was finding.

And then, one day, some lunatic took a chainsaw to her willow. There was a commotion that she couldn't really see from her vantage point, but there was a great deal of magic in the vicinity of her resting place, and then, everything ceased.

Leonora only found out what had actually occurred when Cameron le Fey bridged the place between where Leonora rested and a few of the others. Leonora was thrilled to meet a few of her descendants, but also glad to see Cameron. She'd known his parents in the old days and hadn't seen him since he'd been just a lad. He was a warrior grown now, with potent magical abilities. Somehow, he had become involved with the wolves and Sally's quest to find Leonora's lost descendants.

"Could this be young Cameron? Child of my friends Liandra and Berwid? How fare your parents? You have grown in the many years since I saw you last," she'd said when she'd seen him.

"My parents were well the last time I was in the fey realm. I will tell them you asked, dear lady. Please allow me to make the introductions." He turned smoothly to the two women he'd brought with him. "These are but two of your descendants."

"I've been aware of some, but tell me," Leonora asked, "how many has Sally found?"

"Five have been found, briefed, and have agreed to help," Maria said. "I'm Maria, by the way. I was the first one Sally found, and I mated with Jesse Moore. I live here now."

"Dear Maria," Leonora said, looking at her. "I've felt your presence nearby many times. It's good to see your face, finally. You take after my daughter Marisol, just a little, around the eyes." Leonora was touched by Maria's expression, which held such wonder and compassion. She was a gentle soul.

"And I'm Pam. I just mated with Arlo, and I'm probably going to be living here as well," the other girl said, drawing Leonora's attention.

"Arlo? He's a nice boy. I'm glad to hear he and Jesse have found mates, and I'm especially happy to hear they're part of my extended family now through you two. It's wonderful news! Wonderful!" Leonora was truly happy for the first time since taking refuge inside the willow. Her line would live on, and these two girls, and Sally, were beautiful and kind-hearted.

They talked more about the others who'd been found and where they were living and who they had mated. Leonora was pleased to hear that all of the girls Sally had tracked down so far had found their mates along the way. It boded well for the continuation of dryad energy in the world, even if no full-dryad had been born in eons.

Cameron stood by and watched the proceedings, adding what he knew here and there, but overall, he was just watching them, keeping the spell that allowed this communication active. Leonora hoped it wasn't too tiring for him to hold them all in this hazy half-realm. He was a full-fey warrior, but even he had his limits.

"Fear not, milady." Cameron tried to comfort her as he drew the conversation to a close. "I go now to retrieve the last of your descendants needed to perform the Elven Star ritual. I will guide the magic, and with any luck, it will bring you back into the mortal realm hale and hearty and ready to go another thousand years. Woe be to your enemies, who harmed you so greatly." His smile was almost feral.

"I am in your debt," Leonora replied. "In all of your debt. Please tell the others. I am so grateful for your efforts on my behalf. I cannot wait to walk among you in the forest that is our home."

"And we can't wait to see you there, where you belong," Pam said.

"For now, we must go. Rest easy, milady. Though your resting place was attacked today, it will be guarded much more closely from this moment on. The wolves will keep watch by night and day, now that we know the enemy is aware of your plight," Sir Cameron assured her.

"Tell Master Dmitri that I enjoy his visits, though we cannot speak. I have sensed his presence almost every night. He is a strong ally who keeps his word, and that is much appreciated," Leonora told them.

"I'll be sure to tell him," Maria volunteered. "I'm so glad to see you," she said with feeling that was clearly reciprocated in the dryad's expression.

"Me too," Leonora whispered as Cameron broke the spell, and Leonora faded into the wisps of energy, encased lovingly within the willow.

He had given her hope. So much hope. Although her energy had faded over time, Sally had found six more of her descendants, and when all seven of them had gathered, there might just be enough dryad energy to bring Leonora back to the land of the living.

Chapter One

E arly spring was one of Kaleen Fairchild's favorite times of year. The extensive garden of her parents' suburban home was just starting to come out of its winter slumber, and signs of new life were everywhere.

The crocuses were just finishing, and the daffodils were waving proudly in the brisk air. Tulips were just starting to bloom here and there throughout the large backyard, and trees were starting to form tiny leaves or flowers, each according to their nature. A very old and large oak had pride of place to one side of the wide backyard, with an old swing hanging from its lower branches. There were bushes dividing up the space and an old boxwood hedge along one side separating the rose garden from the rest of the expanse.

Kaleen remembered her father spending many hours out here, coaxing the garden into just the shape and design he wanted. She missed his puttering about back here. Had missed it since she was a child when he disappeared one night, taken by folk from another realm. She'd spent many hours out here ever since, weeding and tilling the soil and planting things in his memory...and in her mother's as well.

They weren't dead. Just gone. And she wasn't sure she'd ever see them again. But she held the hope that one day they would all be reunited, and then, her father would be pleased with how well she'd kept his garden, and her mother would come to enjoy the pink dogwood tree Kaleen had planted just for her.

Kaleen's mother had always claimed the pink dogwood—much rarer than the wild white variety—was her favorite.

It was a bright, sunny day, and the garden was truly waking up. Kaleen was alone, as she always was. The big house was empty, and the garden was her solace. Even on the coldest of days, she always spent at least some time out here among the trees, who were her only friends.

It wasn't a bad life, though it did get lonely at times. Her parents had left her very well off with a big house in a quiet neighborhood. The house was sort of a mansion, really. If a small one. Her nearest neighbors weren't all that close, and they tended to keep to themselves.

Kaleen had been alone here since the day after her eighteenth birthday, though her mother had formulated plans for Kaleen's higher education and set the wheels in motion for Kaleen to attend a nearby college. The money had been there. Plenty of it, actually. Her parents had left her wanting for nothing...except their presence.

Quiet by nature, Kaleen had gone through with the plans her mother had left, getting a degree in accounting. She had a few private clients and did per diem work for a firm in town. All in all, it kept her busy and got her out of the house, but it wasn't exactly fulfilling work. It was just a job that helped her manage the large estate her parents had left behind.

She had been working hard until last week. The April tax deadline had passed, and now, she finally had a little breathing space. The per diem work peaked around the various tax deadlines throughout the year, and her own clients were all set for now. She had taken the next few weeks *off*, though she would still answer the phone if anybody wanted to talk to her. She just wasn't going to be focusing on work as much as she had been since mid-January.

It was a great time to be out in nature, and she felt it calling to her. She'd discovered some unique abilities after her mother had gone, but she had nobody to ask about them. She'd just experimented a bit on her own, playing around out here in her favorite place, making things grow and talking to the trees and bushes.

She knew there was magic in her blood. Her mother had lots of it, after all, but her mother had never told her about listening to the song of the leaves or being able to make things grow just by touching them or the earth around them. That had to be some artifact of her human side, she guessed, but again, she had nobody to ask, so she didn't know for sure. Someday, she might find out. If her parents ever came back.

That melancholy thought came all too often, even after so many years. She missed them. She missed being loved and being able to tell them she loved them. She missed so much about having a family, but she didn't really know how to fix it. As far as she was concerned, her situation couldn't be fixed. She was in a limbo sort of place where she couldn't be with the people she loved unconditionally, and she didn't know how to find others in this world whom she could trust and love just as much.

Which was why she was still alone. She'd tried making friends, but they inevitably let her down. She'd tried dating but had never fallen in love. Lust, certainly. But not love. Much to her regret. She sighed and touched a tulip, causing it to bloom, which made her smile. Her mother had loved tulips.

"Kaleen Fairchild?"

The deep voice jolted her out of her reverie. Kaleen looked up to see a giant of a man staring down at her with intensity in his deep blue eyes. He was tall and lithe, but powerful in the extreme. She jumped to her feet and faced him.

"Who wants to know?" Annoyance peppered her tone.

She wasn't going to be snuck up on in her own garden. How in the world had he managed to do that? Nothing and no one was *ever* able to enter her domain without her knowledge.

"Permit me to introduce myself. Sir Cameron le Fey, at your service."

Shock colored her expression, and she backed up a step involuntarily. "You're fey?"

Cameron tilted his head in question. That wasn't the usual response from those in the mortal realm. He looked at her more closely.

Long blonde hair. Clear blue eyes. Her hair was just a bit darker blonde than usual in fey and her eyes a little darker blue. Still, she had the delicate look of the fey realm, but there was an earthy quality about her too. Could she be part-fey? Half-fey, maybe? Only one way to find out. He had to risk being rude and ask.

"What do you know of the fey realm?"

"Nothing good." She shook her head. "The fey stole my father away." That last was in a whisper that was tinged with both deep sorrow and festering anger.

"Timothy Fairchild. That was your father's name, right?" Something was off here. Something Cameron was puzzling to figure out. This child of the earth should have no knowledge of the fey realm or its denizens.

She looked even more alarmed than when he'd told her his name. "How did you know that?"

Cameron tried to get the conversation back on track.

"I came here at the behest of your cousin, Pamela. Your father's sister's child," he explained patiently. "She sent me here to find you. To put the two of you in contact with each other. And to see if you had inherited your father's earth elemental gifts."

"My father's what?"

She sounded as if she didn't know the first thing about her father's dryad power. Cameron supposed it was possible, given the stories he'd heard about the other part-dryads the Wyoming wolf Pack had found so far.

"Your father had a way with plants, didn't he?" Cameron asked, trying to sound nonchalant but watching her reactions carefully.

"He liked gardening, yes, but I don't see how that—"

Cameron cut her off as gently as possible. There was too much to say and do and too little time to convince her. "Forgive me. Time is of the essence. Your cousin sent me to find you. The rest we can discuss later, but first, I need to pass on her message."

"If what you say is true, why didn't she come here herself?" Kaleen's little chin was stuck up in the air in challenge. Cameron found it endearing, though it wouldn't do to let her know that, just yet.

"Since you seem to have some knowledge of the magical world, have you ever heard of the ancient order known as the *Venifucus*?" Cameron asked in return.

Slowly, she nodded. "An evil order formed by the followers of Elspeth the Destroyer, thought to have died out after she was banished centuries ago."

"I'm very sorry to say, they did not die out. They went into hiding and have recently emerged, still intent on returning Elspeth to this mortal realm. In recent months, they have been targeting those with dryad blood."

"Dryad?" she repeated, interrupting him.

"Earth elementals with power over growing things," he explained quickly. "Our research shows that your father had dryad blood in his heritage, and therefore, so do you. There are several women in your extended family who have only recently come to discover their lineage. They have all been targeted, in one way or another, by those who would seek to destroy them and steal their power. It was feared that you might also come under attack, so I set off to find you. To warn you or intercede on your behalf if you were already in distress."

"The question remains. Why you and not my supposed cousin?" she insisted.

Cameron sighed. "Because she has only just survived being hunted by no less than three very powerful *Venifucus* mages, and she discovered her true mate in the process. I don't know how much you know about shifters, but in the early stages of mating, it is very hard for them to knowingly put their mates in danger. Her new husband is very protective and would not have responded well to the journey here, where you might also come under fire. I volunteered to come after you and hopefully bring you back to them, so you can meet your extended family and get out of the path of danger, should it be pursuing you."

She seemed to consider his words, then looked around her at the peaceful garden, and shook her head.

"As you can see, nobody's pursuing me, as you put it. Except you, maybe." She chuckled at her own words.

"The thing is, though unintentional, the research done to find you might have put you in danger. Since you're part of the family, I don't think anybody would mind me telling you that two of your distant cousins are mated to two very powerful werewolves. Brothers, in fact. The elder brother is Alpha of a large group of ex-military shifters. Have you heard of the Wraiths?"

"The Wraiths?" she repeated his words, a little frown line forming between her eyebrows. "Some kind of shifter mercenary company, I've heard. Legends about them are used to frighten shifter children into good behavior."

"The very same." Cameron grinned a bit at her explanation. "The leader of the Wraiths is an excellent fellow named Jesse. His new mate is a veterinarian named Maria. She is, like you, part-dryad." He nodded toward her. "Jesse's younger brother is Alpha over the larger Pack to which the Wraiths are attached. His name is Jason, and his mate is a former police detective named Sally. She's the one who's been leading the investigation, trying to find the others."

"And her investigation is uncovering other people like me, and somehow putting them in danger?"

"Not intentionally, as I said. But many of the part-dryad women who have been found to date have been in peril. Attacked by *Venifucus* even as Sally was trying to find them. When I left their base, it was feared their communications had been compromised in some way, despite their very best efforts. The entire Pack had been ordered to power down all electronic devices until a thorough security audit could be run by outside specialists they called in just to work on this problem." Cameron shook his head. "As you can imagine, the Wraiths harbor many specialists among their number, so it seems incredible to them that their systems might have been infiltrated. The even more troubling possibility is that someone in the Pack is betraying them. The whole Pack was in a bit of an uproar when I left."

"That doesn't sound good," she agreed cautiously. "So, you think this detective's research might have opened me to the possibility of attack?"

"In a nutshell, yes." Cameron had to hand it to her. She was taking this news rather better than he had expected.

"Well, as you can see, nobody's attacking me right now, so you can just leave." She gestured around the empty garden with her hands outstretched. "You've delivered your warning, and I am warned. Thank you."

"I don't think you understand the gravity of the situation," he began, but she cut him off.

"This is my land. My home. I am well aware of my abilities and have protections all around the place. Nobody can get to me here."

"And yet, I walked right in, and you didn't even know I was here until I said hello." He hated to point that out, but it was the simple truth.

"Ah, yes, but did you intend to do me harm?" She had him there, and the somewhat smug look on her face told him she knew it.

"Of course not. I'm here to help you, not cause more problems."

"Then, I believe my protections are adequate. They are designed to keep evil away from me and my territory." She narrowed her gaze and looked him over. "Though I now believe you mean to help, I don't agree with the need for such assistance."

"Are you familiar with the Elspian Ring?" He had to try to make her understand.

She sighed as if annoyed. "An obsolete piece of magic that only the most powerful of evil sorcerers can produce. Thought to be extinct since the banishing of Elspeth, who invented it."

"Not extinct. I've seen two such workings in just the past few days. In one case, the spell prevented your cousin from knowing that evil mages were prowling through her territory, spying on her homestead. The forest—her friends and early warning system—didn't even see them. The Elspian Ring blocked the regular flow of magic. My point is that each of your distant relatives has faced increasingly more potent magic being used against them. Your cousin had three high-level mages sent against her. At least one of them, and perhaps two, were able to produce a viable Elspian Ring. I saw it myself. I can only imagine what forces they are marshaling to send against you." He shook his head. "Which is why I was sent here. A fey knight with a thousand years of experience fighting evil in the mortal realm. I was here the last time we fought Elspeth. If she has returned—and I, for one, believe she has—then I have pledged an oath to stand with the good people of this realm to fight her and her supporters once again."

Kaleen was silent a moment, looking him up and down. "Only a thousand years?" Her tone was just a bit snide. "My mother's a lot older than you."

Chapter Two

C ameron was blindsided by her statement, but it all sort of clicked into place. Her father might have had dryad blood, but this girl had to be half-fey. Pamela's missing dryad uncle had mated with a fey woman. Goddess' truth! No wonder this slip of a girl knew so much. Her father might have disappeared, but it was clear her mother had taught her a thing or two about magic.

"Who is your mother? For that matter, *where* is your mother?" Cameron asked rather indelicately.

"When my father didn't return after a few years, and I turned eighteen, she went after him. As for who she is, I'm not sure I should tell you. Who are you in the fey realm? Maybe our families aren't aligned. How do I know your kin are not mortal enemies of mine?"

Cameron learned a great deal from that little speech. She had been taught about the political realities of his native realm. That meant she had to come from one of the upper echelon families. Perhaps one of the elite. Perhaps part of the ruling class. Nobility. Which also gave him some idea of where her missing father and mother might be.

"Your father was taken to the fey realm, wasn't he? And your mother waited for his return as long as she could, but decided to go after him once you were old enough to take care of yourself." He shook his head. "I am more than familiar with the political machinations of my own race. I'm sorry for what you've been through. If it's any consolation, your parents will likely one day return here, if they can. I'm sure you know that time passes differently there than it does here. What might take years to transpire here could be only a few days there. And the correlation is not always consistent."

"I am well aware of the capriciousness and vagaries of time translation between here and there. Thank you very much." She sounded so prissy he wanted to pick her up and twirl her about just to see how she would react.

A strange thought. Very unlike himself. Cameron would have to ponder why this little part-dryad, half-fey woman seemed to provoke such strange reactions in him.

"It seems your mother prepared you well for her absence," Cameron allowed. "But tell me, did she realize we were headed toward another confrontation with the Destroyer? From everything you've said, it doesn't sound like it to me."

Kaleen huffed. "She may not have known about every little threat to this realm, but she did her best by me, and I am not concerned. I have handled everything that's come my way since she left, and I will continue to do so. Including you."

Cameron had to hold back laughter. He sensed she wouldn't take his amusement well, and he still had to impress upon her the danger she might be in.

"I'm sorry to say, you should be concerned. Very concerned. The danger is real, and I fear even your skills are not up to the threat. You need allies, little sparrow. And what do you know? Here I am." He opened his arms wide. "Ready and willing to form an alliance."

She eyed him with suspicion. "I'll have to consider it." She put down the small trowel that had been in her hand the whole time they'd been speaking and brushed dirt from her clothing. "But I warn you, I'm a slow decider."

Oh, how he wanted to laugh, but he dared not. This woman was testing him at every turn, sparking his interest with every new interaction. She really was the most fascinating woman he had ever met. And half-fey. Now, that wasn't something he encountered every day in the mortal realm.

So few of his kind could walk the paths between realms. He had been granted special dispensation to do so because of his commitment to the Mother of All. It was by Her grace that he was allowed to cross between the realms at all. And he didn't do it lightly. Only a few times in his long life had he traveled Between.

Kaleen didn't know what to make of the man. He was fey, but he didn't really have the arrogance her mother had taught her to expect. Of course, the only fey Kaleen had ever met in person before had been her mother. Jilial had run from her family to seek refuge in the mortal realm and never looked back...until her family had kidnapped her mate.

Unwilling to take her young daughter on the journey between realms, Jilial had bided her time until Kaleen was old enough to live on her own in the eyes of man. The day after Kaleen's eighteenth birthday, Jilial had taken off to find her beloved husband in the realm of her birth, and Kaleen hadn't seen her since.

She had hope she would see both of them again someday. She knew her mother was doing everything she could to bring Kaleen's father back to the mortal realm and that time worked differently there. Jilial had prepared Kaleen and told her that it might take years of time in this world, but only a few weeks or months might pass in the fey realm. There was no direct correlation. Sometimes, time moved fast. Sometimes, it moved faster. Nobody had yet figured out a formula that could predict it with any accuracy. It would take as long as it took, and then, her parents would come back, if they possibly could.

If not, Kaleen had resigned herself to be content that they were together. As it should be. For they were true mates. Not just some marriage of convenience—which was what her mother's family had tried to force her into accepting. A marriage to some other high-born fey for the sake of building power within the family and accumulating wealth.

Jilial had wanted no part of that. To her, such a marriage would have been torture, for Jilial's tiny touch of second sight had shown her a glimpse of her own destiny centuries ago. A vision of a human man with magical ancestry. Kaleen's father, Timothy. Jilial had risked all to make the perilous journey Between, to meet her fated mate, and her gamble had paid off. She had attained a love the likes of which few ever knew...only to lose him.

Her family had left a note. A nasty message saying that if she wanted her mortal plaything back, she'd have to come and get him. They'd used Timothy as a lure to get her to come back to the fey realm, and Kaleen knew it would be difficult, at best, for them both to get out of there again. But if there was any way possible, they would do it.

So, Kaleen's opinion of the fey was not high. She loved her mother, but she also knew the fey had their own political machinations and power plays. Her mother had fled from her family's control over her life and future and made her own way, but they'd reached out from beyond to mess that up too.

Kaleen didn't want to get involved with any of that. The fey could just stay out of her life, as far as she was concerned. They'd done nothing but mess with her family and cause her to be alone for the better part of two decades.

No. She had no love for the fey. And no desire for this man to stick around any longer than absolutely necessary.

"Well, thank you for your concern, Mr. le Fey, but I have a great deal of work to do," she said, putting her thoughts into action. She wanted to get rid of her troublesome, uninvited guest.

He was just about to object when a new person—a man in a well-tailored suit—walked around the corner of her house and right into her garden, as if he owned the place. What now? And how had two men intruded on her property, right through her wards, in the space of an hour? What was going on here?

"Ah," said the newcomer, smiling in an oily way that put her off immediately. "There you are."

"That's far enough, boy-o," Cameron said, turning to face the new man. "Who are you, and what's your business here?"

The man kept moving forward, unphased by Cameron's confrontational tone. Luckily, the garden was large, and there were the small obstacles of flower beds in the man's way that he needed to skirt around, lest he ruin his fancy leather shoes.

"You can call me Paul," the man said, still smiling in that oozy way as he drew closer, then he raised one hand, and Kaleen saw with horror the blazing blue ball of energy roiling in his palm. "And I'm here to have your power. And your life." He was looking straight at Kaleen when he said it, and she felt a shiver run down her spine.

"Seriously?" she whispered, almost unable to believe this was really happening.

"Oh, I am quite serious, my dear." This time, his words made her shiver. She believed him. He was very serious about hurting her. Possibly killing her.? Possibly? No...*probably.*

Her blood ran cold with fear. She remembered all her mother's advice about magic battles and how the best thing to do was to not get into one in the first place. Kaleen did the first thing she thought of, and ran behind the big oak tree.

That left Cameron out there, facing a lunatic with a growing, glowing blue orb of evil energy in his hands. She felt guilty about that for a split second, but if Cameron was really some kind of fey warrior, he would be able to handle that kind of energy a lot better than she could.

The mage let loose with the energy ball that had grown to the size of a beach ball, and it expanded as it flew through the air toward Cameron. The fey man stood his ground and faced down the mage and his blue energy ball that struck...something. A shield that formed a protective dome over the fey man. Kaleen was fascinated.

The blue energy fell in a perfect circle around the fey man, freezing the ground where it slid off the shield, shriveling any plants in its path, but the fey man remained upright and apparently untouched.

"Shite, that's cold," Cameron said, almost chuckling as he seemed to bait the mage. "So, you're a cold drake, eh? Haven't come across one of you in a very long time, but you'll fall the way they've all fallen when they've chosen the dark path."

He sounded confident, but Kaleen wasn't so sure. That was a lot of magical energy the man had tossed at Cameron, and it was doing terrible damage to her garden! What worse damage could it do to the fey man if his shield failed?

"Nice shield, but it will be you who fall," Paul sneered, advancing slowly on Cameron's position. "How about two at once?" Paul separated his hands, holding glowing blue orbs in each, and lobbed them at Cameron once more.

This time, Kaleen was appalled to note the shrinking of the shield's circumference. As if it couldn't handle the load and had to shrink as it lost power. Then, Paul launched two more, and the shield flickered out with a bright blast of golden energy. For the faintest moment, Kaleen thought she saw glowing, ethereal, golden armor around Cameron. She blinked, and his knightly appearance faded as the armor's glow overpowered her senses.

When she looked again, Cameron was gone. Only a withered and frozen circle of damage remained where he'd been standing. Was he dead?

Kaleen looked around the garden, searching for him and was relieved to find him crouching behind the hedge that separated the rose garden from the rest of the landscaping. She made her way over to him, keeping low and out of sight of the mage who appeared a bit blinded by the intensity of the golden glow.

He was blinking and wiping his eyes, standing in place for the moment. She used the precious minutes to get closer to Cameron.

"Now, do you see what I mean?" he asked her, exasperated as they cowered behind the woody hedge for the moment. "You're in real danger, lass. I can help, but you canna stay here. The enemy knows where you live, and this is just the first attempt to steal your power and end your existence."

"I don't like any of this," she said testily. "Not one bit." She peeked her head around the edge of the hedge to see what Paul was up to. He was spraying the entire garden with blue ice magic. "That bastard is killing my flowers!"

Already the crocus beds were frozen, and the daffodils weren't far behind. The tulips hadn't even really begun to put on their full show of color, and he was killing them before they'd even had time to bloom. The senselessness and evil of his actions brought home to her, like nothing else, that he had to be stopped.

Abruptly, she stood from behind the little cover they had and raised her hands, palms upward. Cameron just shook his head and watched as she put herself in harm's way. Silly sparrow. What did she think she was doing?

She was raising her own shield. That's what she was doing, he realized, after a moment of shocked inertia. If she could manage to distract Paul for even a short amount of time, Cameron might have a chance of ending this the old-fashioned way. He bided his time and waited for his chance.

Sure enough, she raised a shield that was even larger than his had been, though a bit different in nature than his own power. He thought perhaps the plants and trees—and the earth itself—were powering the shield. Handy, that. A dryad must never want for power as long as they were in contact with the earth.

Paul was focused solely on Kaleen now, showering her shield with his murderously cold, icy blue orbs. They were raining down on her dome of protection in a showy display as he moved toward her.

Cameron timed his movements carefully. He was gambling on the idea that Paul didn't know where Cameron was. He snuck around to approach Paul from the side, and conjuring his magical sword, he ran for Paul, using the glowing blade of his Goddess-given weapon to cut right through Paul's shields as if they were made of tissue.

After that, it was easy to cut the man down. The moment Cameron's ethereal weapon touched Paul's skin, he was done for. Not only would the blade cut into his body in the mortal realm, but the magic of this particular weapon—which was not of this earth, but Goddess-derived—cleansed the tainted magic away as if it had never been.

Paul fell to the ground, dead, his magic draining away into the earth, cleansed by the hand of the Divine through the weapon She had gifted Her servant with for just such occasions. Paul, or whoever he really was, lived no more.

"I pray you find your path to the Light in the next realm," Cameron said quietly, looking down at the body. He spoke a benediction for the soul that would live on, even as this body's existence ended.

Kaleen came over, looking down at the dead man. Cameron allowed the sword to go back from whence it had come—a magical Between place known only to the Goddess and Her servants—wiped his hands on his jeans and glanced over at her.

"Good teamwork," he said, feeling the victory of the kill, though of course, he regretted taking another life.

However, his oath to the Goddess meant that he was one of the few beings in the many realms who could do so with a clear conscience. The Mother of All had given him the power and ability to see into a man's heart and soul, for the express purpose of knowing when it was allowable to free the soul to seek a better existence in the next life. This had been exactly such a case. This mage had been too far gone in his own evil. Freeing his soul from this existence at least gave him a chance to find a better way for his spirit the next time around.

Kaleen looked from the dead man to Cameron and back again, then ran for the bushes, where she got noisily, violently ill. Well, that was one reaction, he supposed. It was clear his innocent little sparrow had never seen death before. Not like this.

Cameron regretted having to teach her this horrible lesson, but if things kept going the way he thought they were going, this would be only the first. The greater battle between the forces of good and evil was going to be a lot messier. He'd seen it before. The last time they'd fought Elspeth. It had been a bloodbath. He could only hope the butcher's bill would be somewhat less, this time. Though he had no illusions. It might be that it would turn out to be even worse.

Chapter Three

K aleen felt no better after she tossed her cookies under one of the bushes. She apologized to the bush, but it didn't mind. All organic matter was fertilizer of one kind or another to her green friends. She wasn't sure what the fey warrior would think of her reaction though, and she felt a bit embarrassed.

Of course, it wasn't every day somebody was lobbing cold-fire energy balls in her back garden. And definitely not every day that somebody got killed right in front of her.

All things considered, the man deserved to die for what he'd done to her garden. And what he'd tried to do to her and Cameron.

She was on her hands and knees, next to the bush, her head hung down as she tried to recover at least a little of her dignity. She was also fighting off the last of the dry heaves.

"Are you all right?" Cameron's voice was tinged with concern, and she looked upward a bit to see his shoes parked right in front of her.

She scanned up his legs and torso, then found his face. Yep. He definitely looked concerned. She sat back on her haunches, away from the covering bush and looked at him.

"I'll be fine," she whispered, feeling the rawness of her throat. "Sorry."

"Nothing to be sorry for," he said not unkindly and offered her a hand.

She looked at his big hand for a moment, then decided to trust him. He'd just saved her life—and what was left of her garden. She took his hand and felt a little frisson as his power sparked off hers for a split second, then settled. First-level compatibility among fey. Their magics meshed.

She supposed that was a good thing if she was going to be around him for a while. After this demonstration, she was more likely to follow his lead and go talk to these supposed dryad relatives. If Cameron had wanted to harm her, he'd already had ample opportunity to do so. Chances were, he was on the level.

He helped her get back on her feet, and she left her hand in his much longer than strictly necessary. She couldn't bear to look at the damage done to her garden. Not yet.

"Thank you for your timely intervention," she said formally, not looking away from him. As long as she looked at him, she didn't have to acknowledge the mess that had just been made of her home.

"Thank you for that amazing shield and the distraction it provided," he replied just as formally. "I meant what I said. We make a good team."

"I'm not much of a fighter, and I've never raised a shield like that before. It just felt like something I could try after I saw what you had around you," she explained, trying to hide the tears that threatened now that she was in the aftershock of battle. She'd never *been* in battle before, and she was starting to feel a bit shaky.

"You did just the right thing, lass. You have very good instincts," he complimented her.

"I think I need to sit," she told him as her knees gave out, but he was there to catch her before she could fall.

She liked being held in his strong arms. She felt like a doll next to his large size, though she was tall for a woman. He made her feel delicate, and there was genuine care and maybe...respect...in his touch.

"All right, little sparrow," he almost crooned. "You just sit here for a bit. There's more I need to do to prevent this character from ever bothering us again." He placed her on the bench beneath the old oak tree. She felt better already, being near her home oak. It reached out its energy to her in concern, and she felt absurdly grateful for its presence.

"You mean he's not dead?" she asked as the possible meaning of his words penetrated her fogged mind.

"No, I assure you, he's quite dead, but I need to do a few things to make absolutely certain that he stays that way. When you're dealing with mages as evil as this one, it pays to dot all the I's and cross all the T's." He stood and surveyed the wreckage of her garden, then nodded. "I need to make a magical pyre, and the big spot over there that was cold-burned will do, and it won't cause any further damage."

He set off with determination. The first thing he did, though, was kneel over the body and search the man's pockets very thoroughly. He kept the wallet and keys and a few other things. Then, he dragged the man's body to the nearby spot that was already damaged and stood back.

Cameron waved his hands in the air in a very specific pattern that she sort of half-recognized from her mother's teachings. He was putting up protective wards first. She recognized that much, but after that, he lost her. His magic was very advanced, and she thought she heard a few words of High Fey being muttered just at the edge of her hearing. Cameron had more than a few very impressive tricks up his sleeve, it seemed.

A moment later, a magical flame erupted and consumed the mage who had called himself Paul in under thirty seconds. He was there, then he was gone. Dissolved into molecules to be reabsorbed by the earth from which all things came.

Kaleen felt the passage of the man's energies into the earth, never to return and forever cleansed of the evil taint. She felt lighter. Freer. Cameron had been correct to do this rite. She felt it deep in her bones.

Well, that was one thing taken care of. The evil mage was no more, and he would not be returning to haunt them, but her garden was in dire shape. It would take a long time to fix, even with her special talent with growing things.

Dryad, he had called her. It sort of made sense, all things considered. She wondered why the thought had never occurred to her before now. Of course, as a High Court fey, her mother had possessed a lot of really spectacular magic, and as Kaleen's abilities developed, they'd just put it up to that. She wondered if her father had ever realized he had a way with plants because he had dryad blood?

Probably not, or her mother would have mentioned it. But the idea that both of her parents had magic gave them both a much better shot at surviving the ordeal they were no doubt being put through in the fey realm. Her father wasn't just some powerless mortal sucked into the political games of the fey court. He had power of his own. She just hoped his elemental power could help him wherever he was now.

Cameron watched over the pyre until it fizzled out, leaving no trace behind of the evil mage. Then, the fey warrior walked over to the bench under the oak and calmly looked at her.

"How are you doing now, lass?" he asked, that touch of concern still in his voice.

"Much better, thank you," she said. "And thank you for...cleaning up," she said, swallowing the bile in the back of her throat. She still couldn't quite believe she'd been attacked in her own home, in the garden that had given her such solace for so many years.

"It was the least I could do, under the circumstances." He looked around then zeroed back in on her face. "I don't think it's really safe for you here anymore. Not at the moment anyway. The enemy knows where you are, and this man was only the first they sent against you. There will be more. Mark my words."

"I'm not going to argue with you any further," she told him with a sigh. "It's clear you know a lot more about the current situation than I do. I'm sorry I was so foolish before. I should have listened to you."

Tears gathered behind her eyes, but she refused to let them fall. She was through acting the weakling. She had to get herself together. She was her mother's daughter, and she would fight for what was right. That was encoded in her very DNA.

She was shocked into meeting his gaze when he took her hand in his. She read compassion and some kind of flame in the depths of his eyes. A flame of...attraction? No. She had to be imagining things.

"Don't beat yourself up. This is a unique situation. I didn't expect you to just believe me instantly and take off for Wyoming with me."

"Wyoming? Is that where they are? The other part-dryads, I mean."

"Aye," he confirmed softly. "They live on a mountain there. The whole Pack and the subset that are the Wraiths and their families."

"The Wraiths have families?" She was surprised by that.

If she'd thought about them at all, she would have assumed a shifter mercenary company would be comprised of loners who had no ties. Then again, they were shifters. Her mother had told her how important it was for certain types of shifters to run with their Packs. Particularly wolves.

"Quite a few of them do," Cameron replied. "Though, the Wraiths live on top of the mountain, somewhat apart from the rest of the Pack, who occupy the lower slopes of that same mountain. It's a very big Pack."

"And two of my supposed cousins are there?" she prompted him.

"Aye. And the dryad from whom you all descend is trapped in a willow tree on that same mountain, fighting for her life. It is to free her that Sally began the task of tracking you all down, once she became aware that there were more women out there like herself. She, and a number of the others, didn't grow up knowing of her power or where it came from."

"But they knew about magic, right? I mean, once the power started flowing through them... It would be pretty hard to ignore, I think." She tried to imagine what it would be like to know nothing about the existence of magic and then suddenly have it at your fingertips. Probably very confusing.

"I suspect so, but from what I understand, quite a few of them lived in the mortal world and had no idea that Others existed," he explained. "You should talk to them. I know they want your help in freeing your ancestor. Six part-dryads have been identified so far. You are the seventh. If you agree, we can attempt the Elven Star. Do you know of it?"

Kaleen nodded, gulping. "It is ancient and potent, according to my mother's teachings. I have never attempted such a powerful working, but if it's for a good cause, then I would be willing to try."

Cameron gave her a broad smile. "I have done such workings. Not often and not lightly, but I have done them. It is my intent to help walk the ladies through the spell and be there to help, should my help be needed. Leonora—your ancestor—is an old friend of my parents, and I have known her since childhood. I would like to see her restored to health and the forest that she loves."

Kaleen considered him for a moment. He was very convincing and sounded sincere. And she owed him after what he'd just done to save her life. Plus, she really didn't think it was safe to stay here. What he'd said was correct. The enemy knew where she lived now, and until the threat was eliminated, she was in danger.

Though, exactly how to eliminate that threat remained a mystery to her. First things first. She had to just take this mess a step at a time. Wyoming. For now, she would go to Wyoming and try to help her supposed ancestor and meet these other part-dryads. If they truly were part of her extended family on her father's side, she would be pleased to know them. She'd had no ties with her father since he'd been stolen away. It might be good to make contact with his people.

After all, they were really her people too. It would be nice to have family again, even if they were relative strangers. She almost laughed at her own pun. Relatives who were strangers. Fitting.

"All right. I'll go to Wyoming, if that's what you're offering, and see what I can do to help with this great magical working you propose. After that, I guess I'll just have to see. It's clear I can't stay here right now, but I do despair for the garden." She looked around at the mess again and tried hard to hold in her emotions.

Cameron squeezed her hand. "It will be all right, lass," he whispered, moving a little closer. "Please don't look so sad."

Tears gathered behind her eyes. He was being so kind and had been so incredibly brave. She looked up into his eyes, and he moved closer still.

"You make me want to kiss the sadness away," he breathed, his mouth coming closer to hers.

She was frozen. She hadn't been kissed in far too long and never by such a powerful male. Never by a fey. Or a warrior. Suddenly, she wanted nothing more than to know what Cameron's kiss would feel like. She moved infinitesimally closer until their lips touched.

And then, the world spun out of control. Or at least, that's how it felt. His lips claimed hers, and all sense fled from her mind. All she could do was enjoy.

He put his arms around her, and she relished the feel of his embrace as he deepened the kiss. Unexpected, but not unwelcome, his kiss made her feel *alive* in a way she hadn't felt...possibly ever. No other kiss she had ever received could compare to this one.

Kaleen put her hands on his shoulders, then moved them up around his neck as the kiss went on. But all good things had to end, and this interlude ended far too soon for her tastes.

After releasing her lips, Cameron trailed kisses along her jaw. He eased away little by little until he finally moved back enough to look deep into her eyes.

"Should I apologize for that, little sparrow?" His voice was deep, rich and intimate in the silence of the backyard.

"I don't think so," she replied softly, trying to get her bearings.

The world as she had known it had just changed in the most delicious way. She wasn't sure if she ever wanted it to go back to the way it had been. She wouldn't have missed the sensations she'd just experienced for the world. And she wanted to do it again, but now was not the time. Clearly.

Her beloved garden was in ruins, some unknown enemy appeared to be gunning for her, and the most intriguing man she had ever met was looking at her expectantly. She had made her decision. She was going to trust him and go with him to meet these purported dryads. It was safer than staying here at the moment. Because, she had no doubt he was telling the truth. Paul was only the first. There would be more people like him coming to kill her and steal her power.

That was something her mother had always warned her about. A full-grown fey with centuries of experience, her mother hadn't had to worry too much about anyone attacking her that she couldn't handle. Her daughter, on the other hand, had limitations. She was half-human, after all, and had very little experience with the magical world.

Her mother had tried to train her as she grew, knowing the day would come when her mother would have to leave her on her own in the mortal realm. It was the only way. Her mother had impressed that upon her long ago. If they ever wanted to be a family again, her mother was going to have to go and get her father back.

It was a great risk. Risky for her mother, who might not ever be able to return from the fey realm. Risky to leave a young half-fey girl on her own in a world that mostly didn't believe in magic. But without risks, they could not reap the rewards.

And now, here was Cameron. With another set of risks. Kaleen trusted herself and her judgment enough by now to think it was worthwhile to take the risk of going with him. Especially since the risk of staying here was much greater.

But, if she was going to leave, there were a few things she wanted to take with her. She stood from the bench, waiting a moment to make sure her feet would stay under her, then started walking toward the house. Cameron followed.

She'd seen the concern on his handsome face, but she hadn't been able to put into words all that she had been thinking. Her mind was still a little scrambled from that kiss. He would figure it out soon enough when he saw her packing.

She needed a change of clothes, and probably a shower, if she had time. All that running about in the garden had left stains on her clothing and wiped her out energetically. A hot shower would go a long way toward restoring some of her equilibrium.

She entered the back door of the house, Cameron following not far behind. They were in the kitchen, and she went directly to the cupboard where she kept the reusable shopping bags she took with her when she went to the market. They would do to carry some of the things she would bring with her.

Chapter Four

"How much time do you think we have?" Kaleen asked Cameron, turning toward him. "I mean, do I have enough time to take a quick shower and pack some things, or should we make a run for it?"

"We probably have time for that," he assured her. "Can I help in any way?"

A naughty thought entered her mind as she considered him *helping* her in the shower, but that's probably not what he'd meant. She schooled herself to stop thinking such scandalous thoughts and tossed him the little bag of rolled up grocery bags.

"I assume we're going on a road trip, right?" she asked.

He nodded. "That's how I got here. My vehicle is parked not too far away."

"Good. Then please pack the perishable foods into those bags. Whatever you think we could eat on the road. It's not going to do me any good turning to slime in the refrigerator while I'm gone." She made a face at the thought of the mess. "There's fresh bread and cold cuts. Maybe you could slap a few sandwiches together?"

"I most certainly can," he replied at once, smiling. "To be honest, I'm getting a little tired of fast food. I should have thought to pack provisions before I started out to find you."

"Excellent. I'll just run upstairs, pack a few things, and grab a quick shower." She was already on her way out of the kitchen when another thought occurred.

"If you wouldn't mind checking all the windows and doors to make sure they're locked, I'd appreciate it. I have an alarm system, and I'll be putting that on once we're ready to leave, but it pays to check everything."

"Agreed. I will be glad to help make your home secure," he said, bowing his head slightly to the side in an old-world show of respect and agreement.

"Thank you." She headed upstairs without further delay.

She needed to pack some clothes, but there were also some magical items she needed to secure for the journey. Things her mother had entrusted to her that must not be left behind for the enemy to find.

Cameron felt odd. He'd just kissed the sparrow and felt not one bit of guilt over it. He looked down at his forearm, at the mating mark that he'd carried for a thousand years. It was all the he had left of the mortal woman he had loved and tried to keep with him for as long as possible. Molly, her name had been.

She'd been a dark-haired temptress, full of passion and light. She had burned bright, as most mortals did, but all too fast. He'd marked her with this fey magic, and it had extended her life long past where most mortals left this realm, but she had left him, nonetheless. She had loved him, but in the end, she had told him they were not meant to be. They'd enjoyed a hundred years together, but she had died in his arms, bidding him to move on with his life and find love again.

He'd refused. For centuries, he'd refused to entertain the idea that he could love anyone else. He'd embraced the warrior lifestyle offered by the Goddess as one of Her Knights of the Light. He'd lived only to serve and had forsaken his fey heritage. He hadn't even looked at another woman with more than a passing lust, quickly sated...until today.

They mating mark on his arm seemed to pulse slightly and when the pulse ended, the mark seemed fainter to his magical sight than it had been before. He wasn't sure what that meant, but he also wasn't sure he liked it. Change was difficult for him. It always had been.

Fey, in general, with their near-immortal lifespans found it hard to accept change. Living in the mortal realm had helped Cameron begin to accept such things, but he'd kept himself somewhat apart from the world he lived in, never really engaging on an emotional level.

For the first time in a long time, today, his emotions had become engaged. He lowered his arm and set to work, shaking his head. Few others in the mortal realm could see the golden circle that was a magical tattoo on his arm. Nobody would know what it meant unless he told them.

The kiss he had bestowed on the sparrow was some kind of aberration. A simple kindness to a young woman who had been through a great trauma. He was here to help her, and help her he would. Which meant he had to get to work.

He felt very domestic, making sandwiches in Kaleen's kitchen. She had an economical setup. Small, but well organized, and he was able to find everything he needed in short order. He loaded one of the nylon bags with all the things that would go bad in the fridge that he couldn't quite use right away, then filled another with sandwiches and snack items he found in her cupboards and refrigerator.

He found vegetable sticks of various kinds ready to go, so he snagged a bottle of dressing to go with and put that in one of the insulated bags he found tucked away in another cupboard. They were going to eat well on their journey. Much better than he had coming out here.

He kept thinking about that kiss and realized he probably shouldn't have done it. However, she hadn't objected, and he couldn't seem to help himself. It had been a very long time, indeed, since he'd been unable to control his impulses.

His mother would frown if she knew. His father would probably just shake his head, though really, how could Cameron resist? Kaleen was so appealing—albeit she was half-human. But her human half also held her dryad ancestry. She was truly a child of two worlds.

His parents would probably have grave concerns over such a woman. They'd see her as a wildcard and unsuitable as a match for one of their sons, but Cameron was far down the hierarchy enough that he didn't really have to listen to their edicts. Especially not since he'd sworn his oath to the Mother of All. His status as a Knight of the Light made all other considerations moot. That duty took precedence over all others—familial, political—it didn't matter. The Goddess came first, no matter what, and she outranked everyone, up to and including his illustrious parents. Though he knew his mother would worry. Marrying a mortal was one of the oldest recipes for heartache among fey kind.

He'd already done that and suffered the loss for centuries. He wasn't going to succumb again. His mother need not worry. He wasn't going to marry Kaleen. He wasn't even going to get involved with her. One little kiss under a charming, sheltering oak did not a relationship make.

He ignored the little voice in his head that said they'd be on the road together for a couple of days at least. A lot could happen in a couple of days, but he wouldn't allow it.

They were on a mission to get Kaleen to her family in Wyoming as quickly and safely as possible, then help them all restore Leonora to health. That was it. There would be no more flirtation. No more attraction. And definitely, no more kissing.

Cameron tried really hard to get his mind back on track, but just at that moment, the water turned on upstairs, and he knew she was in the shower, or soon would be. Naked. With warm water sluicing down her lithe body.

Sweet Mother of All. He had to get a grip on his wayward thoughts.

Finished with the food prep for their journey, he went through all the downstairs rooms to make sure the windows were locked and anything electronic that might cause some kind of issue was unplugged. He thought about checking the upstairs windows, but the shower was still running, and he figured it would be safer for him to wait until Kaleen was downstairs, so he wouldn't be tempted to further their acquaintance in the most carnal way.

Down, boy.

He was going to have to travel in a small vehicle for a couple of days with this woman. He had to tamp down the urge to kiss her and do...other things. He wasn't some wet-behind-the-ears boy who was desperate for a woman. Truth be told, he hadn't been with a lass in quite some time, but that didn't mean anything. As he'd grown older, he'd become more circumspect in his liaisons and a bit pickier about the kind of woman he would bed.

Since losing Molly, he'd broken more than one human heart, and he refused to do that again. It just wasn't fair to the women. By the same token, he wasn't ready to settle down with some fey woman. He wasn't ready to go back home for good yet, if he ever would be. He had a sacred duty, and it was one that he enjoyed. It was important to him to fight evil wherever it showed its ugly face, and if the big blow up he expected was on its way, he needed to be right where he was, in the mortal realm, ready to help.

Right now, his duty had taken him to this startling part-dryad. The fact that she was half-fey had been completely unexpected.

The water cut off upstairs, and he returned to the kitchen. He heard her rummaging around upstairs for a few minutes as he cleaned up the spot on the counter where he'd been working earlier. He was just finishing up when he heard her come downstairs.

"I'm just going to pack a few things from my office, and then, we can go, but I was wondering if there was time to maybe call my cousins before we head out. I'd like to at least talk to them. I was thinking maybe something would spark—magically, I mean—to let me know I'm heading in the right direction," she explained, looking a little nervous.

All that time alone must have brought doubt to her mind. Cameron understood. She was wise to be cautious.

He nodded. "The sooner we get going, the better, but I can arrange a call. You go pack, and I'll get one or both of them on the line, if possible."

She nodded and went off to do her packing while he pulled out his smartphone. He dialed the Pack Alpha's number. It was only right to go through him where his mate was concerned. Shifters liked their protocol—some species more than others. Wolves were among those who relied heavily on the Pack structure and traditions, and Cameron wasn't going to mess with that.

By the time Kaleen was back to the kitchen, Cameron had both Sally and Maria on a video call. He gave the phone to Kaleen, briefly making the introductions. Then, he backed off and watched the interaction.

If he was any judge, he'd say the women hit it off right away. Sally took the lead, explaining how she'd tracked Kaleen down and apologizing if her inquiries had put Kaleen in jeopardy. Kaleen didn't go into detail but related the fact that she had been attacked in her own back garden, but Cameron had been there to save the day.

All in all, she was taking it rather well, and he saw renewed confidence as she got to know her cousins a little. She looked much better after the shower. The pallor of shock was gone, and she looked livelier than she had. Fey were usually quite pale, but she'd been paler than most after the ordeal in the garden.

When she ended the call a few minutes later, she handed Cameron's phone back to him with vague thanks as she nodded to herself. She looked so adorably pensive, he wanted to kiss her again. Of course, he'd been fighting that instinct for a while now. It seemed all she had to do was breathe and he wanted to pick her up and kiss the living daylights out of her. He shook his head just slightly, reminding himself to behave.

"Where are your bags?" he asked a little more gruffly than he'd intended. That seemed to shake her out of her reverie, and she looked up at him.

"I just have a duffel bag for clothes and a soft briefcase with my laptop and a few important papers." She pointed to the two bags that were sitting just inside the doorway.

"Do you want me to check the windows upstairs?" Cameron offered.

"Already done. Thanks. We're good to go, I think." She sounded much more confident than she looked, but the call with her cousins had helped overall, he believed.

"Right-o." He grabbed her duffle bag, but she held tight to her soft briefcase.

Cameron shrugged and retrieved the bags from the kitchen counter with the food. He loaded everything across his back in a jury-rigged strap arrangement he'd concocted to leave his arms as free as possible while they walked the short distance to where he'd parked his vehicle.

With a last look around her home, Cameron watched as Kaleen locked the door and then shook her head. She sighed heavily and then roused her spirits with visible effort.

"See you again soon, house," she whispered, then added a Word of protective magic that sealed the place even more securely than the mundane locks.

Turning resolutely away from her home, she followed his lead to where he'd parked. They made it there safely, and he quickly disengaged the bags on his back, stowing them in order of need. The bag of sandwiches he put within easy reach. Her duffel bag of clothes went in the very back, alongside his own overnight bag.

She climbed into the passenger seat and made herself comfortable. Cameron started the engine, and they were on their way. It was some miles before she spoke.

"I'm glad you were able to arrange that video call with my cousins. Thank you," she said softly.

"You're very welcome," he replied at once. "There's a bit of a communications blackout where they are at the moment. The Pack is looking for the leak in their coms that allowed the enemy to hack into Sally's investigations. It's hard to know what's safe, but I figured the enemy already knows where you live, so you might as well have a conversation with them before we move on."

She nodded. "Sound reasoning, though I don't like the idea that anybody like that knows where I live."

Cameron sighed. "I know. It's not pleasant in the least, but with any luck, we can draw the attention away from you, and you can return home later, under safer conditions." He didn't really know how that might come about, just yet, but he'd strive for that result, if at all possible.

"I liked them. Sally and Maria," she explained as she looked out the windshield at the road ahead. They were on the highway now, heading west. "I can't really explain it, but the minute I saw them, I felt a sort of kinship with them."

"That's good," he told her. "I'd hoped you would have some kind of recognition. Your magic derives from the same place—from Leonora—so it makes sense that you would recognize each other." Cameron tilted his head, considering. "Though, of course, you also have a great deal of fey blood, which gives your magic a different flavor. But the influence of the dryad has been strong in all her progeny that I've met. Leonora is a force of nature. You'll see when you meet her."

"Have you known her long?" He felt her watching him.

"She knows my parents and first met me when I was a child. Well over a thousand years ago by the counting of the mortal realm," he admitted. "So, I guess you would say we've known each other a very long time." His lips quirked up in a grin, and he glanced over at her, but she was frowning.

"I know of such things, of course, but it's still odd to hear you speak so casually of living for eons. I've only ever lived here, and I expect I've aged like a normal human being, despite being half-fey. I don't expect to live too much longer than the average shifter. What is that? A few hundred years? That's all I suppose I'll get. The fey blood is there, but it's not *all* that's there."

"True," he agreed. "But you're not fully human on your father's side, either. The dryad magic has to be taken into account, though what effect it will have on your longevity is hard to predict.

"I don't get it," she admitted, turning back to contemplating the road in front of them. "What use is being able to make plants grow and hear the song of the trees? That doesn't seem like much compared to what I know my mother can do with her fey magic."

"The power of the dryad is the power of an earth elemental," he told her, in all seriousness. "Elemental magic is some of the oldest, most powerful magic there is in this or any other realm. Do not discount it."

She seemed to think of that for a few moments, then shrugged. "If you say so." She found the lever that would recline her seat a little bit and leaned back, shutting her eyes. "I'm going to rest for a bit if you don't mind. It seems I've had a big day."

He chuckled at her wry humor and concentrated on his driving. They had many miles to go before he could sleep.

Chapter Five

K aleen woke after only an hour or two of dozing when Cameron pulled off the road. He parked them in an open corner of a large lot belonging to a busy truck stop. They got out and stretched their legs.

"I'm going to use the ladies' room," she told him.

"Don't linger, and if you buy anything in the store, use cash only," he warned her before he let her go. You can be traced if you use credit cards."

She hadn't really thought about that, and it drove home the serious situation in which she found herself. She nodded at him and walked toward the entrance of the truck stop, the fact that enemies might be trying to pick up her trail troubled her greatly.

She didn't waste time and was back at the vehicle a few minutes later. She'd used cash to buy a few sodas and some candy bars. She offered to share her bounty with Cameron, and he raised one ginger eyebrow at her before taking one of the packages.

"Got a bit of a sweet tooth, have you?" he asked as he tore into the wrapper and bit off a piece of twisted red licorice.

"I guess so," she replied. "Especially when I'm nervous or stressed."

He tossed the remainder of the licorice onto his seat and looked at her. "Will you be all right if I run in there for a minute? I think we're safe enough for now. I haven't sensed anything scrying us, though that's not a perfect guarantee.

Still, I don't think the enemy has had time to find you yet and mount a second attempt."

"I'll be fine. You go ahead," she assured him.

Oddly, as he jogged away, she felt less confident. He had saved her earlier, and she had apparently come to count on him to make her feel safe. Weird. She'd been self-sufficient for so many years. It seemed strange that this red-headed giant should come into her life and become so necessary to her feeling secure in such a short amount of time.

He was back quickly, and they ate some of the sandwiches he'd made before getting back on the road. She offered to drive, but he claimed he enjoyed it, so she hopped back into the passenger seat.

"We don't have vehicles like this in the fey realm. I love driving internal combustion engines, which is one of the big draws for me to stay here, in the mortal realm," he volunteered as they drove along. "It was different when I first came here, of course. I fought Elspeth the first time she threatened this realm. I really like how technology has progressed since then." He smiled and patted the steering wheel. "I like motorcycles too."

"Those things are dangerous," Kaleen told him, with a shiver. "One of our neighbors had a son who died in a motorcycle accident. He was a nice boy. They say there's no small accident with a motorcycle." She had liked that boy. She'd wanted to date him when she was old enough, but he'd died shortly before her sixteenth birthday.

Cameron looked over at her and nodded. "I'm sorry for your loss." He seemed to temper his enthusiasm. "I always exercise due caution, I assure you."

She watched the miles pass, and they stopped once more to use the restrooms in a much smaller travel stop on the side of the road. She wanted to know more about the war with Elspeth back in the Dark Ages, but she didn't know how to ask. He probably had bad memories from those days, and she didn't want to stir them up.

She also wanted to know more about the dryads and the people they were going to meet in Wyoming, but she found that hard to talk about as well. Instead, she stuck to the weather and road conditions like a big ninny.

This was the most adventure she'd ever had, and she was feeling a bit out of her depth. Most of her days were spent at home, working on her computer in a darkened room. She had her garden, and she went out occasionally to buy groceries or shop for other things, but she didn't have a lot of friends and spent most of her time alone.

Now, here she was, on a road trip to visit relative strangers with one of the most intriguing and attractive men she'd ever met. She didn't know quite what to make of it all now that she had some time to think. He was good company. Quiet when she needed quiet to get her thoughts in order. Talkative when she asked questions or wanted to chat. She noticed he wasn't asking any prying questions either, so she supposed she was taking her cues on that from him. But she'd be disappointed if they got to their destination without her learning anything more of substance about him.

He intrigued her. His ruddy good looks and imposing stature were attractive, but it was his keen intellect that really made her want to plumb the depths of his nature. His height made her feel delicate, though she'd always been tall for a woman. None of the boys she'd known in school had ever made her feel small by comparison.

Cameron wasn't just tall, but broad shouldered, and that shock of red hair was both striking and very, very sexy. His blue eyes felt like lasers, boring into her, scanning everything and leaving no secret uncovered. It was ridiculous, of course, but when he looked at her—really looked at her—she felt exposed. And not necessarily in a bad way.

After dark, Cameron chose a seemingly random hotel just off the highway to stop. He went into the office and got them a room while she stayed in the car. The fewer people who saw her, he said, the better. She supposed he was right, and she was really too weary to argue by that point. All she wanted was a soft place to lay her weary head.

The hotel was nothing special, and he'd arranged for a room on the first floor on a far corner of the building. There was a side door through which they could enter without having to go through the lobby, so they parked the vehicle close to that entrance and used it to get into the room.

She was pleased to find that the room had two double beds, as well as a small desk area, a little table and a fridge. The coffeemaker was tiny, but adequate to brew about two cups at a time.

"The refrigerator is a marvelous invention of your modern era," Cameron observed as he stowed the bag still full of sandwiches in little baggies in the mini-fridge. "We could order a pizza for dinner, just to have a change of pace from the sandwiches," he offered. "I saw an advertisement in the lobby and asked the desk clerk if it was any good, and he gave them a high recommendation."

"Sure, I love pizza," she replied easily. They went on to discuss what toppings they might prefer, and within a few minutes, Cameron dialed the pizzeria's number from the hotel phone and placed the order.

Kaleen was getting over her awkwardness at being alone in a hotel room with a virtual stranger. Especially, a stranger she was very attracted to. Cameron was simply a man out of her experience. Fully fey, he was much more mysterious to her than she had imagined. The only fey she had ever met was her own mother. Cameron was nothing like her.

Kaleen's mother was a tall willowy blonde. Even paler than Kaleen, her skin was almost translucent and perfect in every way. No blemish would dare go near her mother's skin, Kaleen had always thought with an inward smile. Her hair was so pale as to be almost white. A champagne blonde, that's what they called her, and it was completely natural. Her mother's eyes were blue, but a pale blue that was more of an icy gray.

Kaleen was a slightly darker version of her mother, with golden blonde hair, blue eyes, and a curvy, more human form. Kaleen had always assumed that other fey would look more like her mother. Those ethereal features—high cheekbones, perfect skin, pale eyes, etc. She had also assumed they would be tall and skinny.

Cameron had the tall part, but he was far from thin. His bulk wasn't fat, either. He was pure muscle. Clearly, a warrior. And his coloring was more ruddy than pale. Kaleen found, much to her surprise, she liked that very much.

Being alone with him for so many hours, she had thought she'd gotten a bit used to being around him. But stopping for the night presented a whole new series of challenges. They weren't just sitting side-by-side in a moving vehicle. That was comfortable, by now. That was easy.

No, now, they were face-to-face, in a small room whose dominant feature was two very large, very inviting beds. It was kind of hard to ignore, but she made a valiant effort.

The pizza arrived, and Cameron paid the delivery person in cash. Kaleen offered to split the cost, but he insisted on paying.

After shutting the door tight and locking it, he put the pizza down on the small table near the window. He took the chair, and she sat on the side of the bed closest to the window as they ate. They had covered a lot of miles that day, in addition to the nastiness that had occurred at her home. She was tired. Bone tired, despite the napping she had done while he drove.

"It seems the desk clerk did not lie," Cameron observed after taking a big bite of his slice of pizza. "This is delicious. What do you think?"

She nodded as she chewed and then swallowed. "Yes, it's very good. Some of the best I've ever had, I think."

They talked companionably about the pizza, and other foods that they liked in common, while they ate. When she finished her first slice of pizza, she was ready to get cleaned up. Cameron looked like he would probably eat several more slices, so she rose and went to her bag, collecting the things she might need.

"Do you mind if I take the bathroom first? I'd like to freshen up a bit and change into my pajamas. It's amazing how tired I get from just traveling. I never thought sitting still for so long could be so exhausting." She smiled, trying to hide the fact that her nervousness was returning.

It's not that her pajamas were revealing in any way, but they *were* pajamas. Intimate. Thin fabric that didn't seem like much protection. What she needed protecting from, she wasn't sure. She didn't think Cameron would take advantage of her in any way.

Even if she wanted him to.

He'd been the perfect gentleman since they'd met earlier that day. It seemed like a lifetime ago. In that short span of time, she had come to trust him with her life. He had already saved it once. That alone had earned him her respect.

"Sure," he replied, then took a sip of his soft drink. "You might as well. I'll leave a slice for you," he added with a grin.

She smiled back. "Thanks."

For the second time that day, Cameron waited outside a bathroom, knowing that Kaleen was getting naked in there. *Uncomfortable* didn't begin to cover the way he was feeling. She was the most unconsciously alluring woman he had ever met, and the more he was around her, the more he was attracted to her.

It was impossible, of course. His oath to the Goddess and the way he chose to live his life since losing Molly didn't leave room in it for a woman of any kind, much less someone so tied to the mortal realm. Not that he intended to live the rest of his life in the fey realm. As far as he was concerned, his family was doing quite well without him there and would manage. But that didn't mean he never wanted to go back there, ever. He loved his brothers and sisters. He respected and loved his parents. He wouldn't want to go the rest of his life without ever seeing them again.

Cameron had always known that, if he chose another mortal mate, he would not only be setting himself up for repeated heartbreak, but he wouldn't be able to visit his family. The difference in the time flows between this realm and the fey realm made it impossible to predict how long one might be gone if they went Between. The Goddess guided his travels when he was on missions for Her, but he couldn't count on that always being the case. There was a reason the mortal realm was not overrun with fey, and vice versa. It wasn't that easy to go Between.

So, he had to fight against this attraction. She was the most beautiful, brave, witty, and desirable woman he had met, but there could never be anything significant between them. He had a feeling she was the kind of woman who didn't give out her favors easily or with no thought to the future. If she gave herself, she would give her heart—at least partially—as well. Cameron didn't want to cause her problems. And he definitely didn't want to break her heart. He liked her too much to do that.

Cameron demolished the rest of the pizza, leaving the largest slice for Kaleen. He could just hear her moving about in the bathroom, the water running and then turning off a few times. Tonight was going to be interesting. Highly magical, he didn't always need that much sleep. He would stand watch over her while she slept, and try not to think about how much he wanted her.

He stood as she came out of the bathroom and tidied up the pizza box. He left the single slice on a paper plate for her and tossed the rest of the debris into the trashcan.

"I'm going to take a quick shower," he told her. "Don't answer the door for anything, and if you need me, just knock on the bathroom door, and I'll be right with you."

She nodded her agreement, already starting on her second piece of pizza. He studiously ignored the soft black material of her pajamas. They might be considered conservative, by some, but the way the dark fabric set off her pale skin and golden hair unnerved him a bit. Not to mention, the way the thin fabric hugged every curve and left very little to his imagination.

Cameron hightailed it into the bathroom, turning the shower on and opting for cold water. At least, for the moment. He had to get himself under control before he went back out there. It wouldn't do to let her see just how much he desired her.

She was still in danger, despite the fact that he had seen no pursuit today. He couldn't let his guard down. He couldn't take his eye off the ball. He was here to protect her and get her safely back to Wyoming. He had to keep that in mind. Dalliance wasn't an option.

Focusing his mind, and controlling his body, he took a brief shower then changed into sweats. They were comfortable to sleep in and could be worn outside as well. A compromise over wearing his cargo pants with the many pockets. They were still somewhat new, and a bit scratchy. He would put them on in the morning, though, because he preferred to travel with all of the bits of equipment he had in those pockets on his person.

When he left the bathroom a few minutes later, Kaleen was already in bed. She had claimed the bed closest to the window, leaving him the bed nearer the door. The arrangement satisfied him. The window didn't open, so the likelier point of entry, if someone found them, would be the door.

Cameron propped himself up against the headboard and contemplated the rest of his mission. They had a ways to go yet to get to Wyoming, but so far, the trip had gone well. Better than expected, actually. He sent a prayer to the one he served that they would continue to have safe travels, then returned to his planning. He most definitely was not going to think about the beautiful woman laying soft and warm in a bed not even five feet away from him. Nope. No siree. That would not do at all.

Chapter Six

K aleen woke up in the middle of the night, confused for a moment by the strange surroundings. In a rush, memory returned. She rolled over and could just make out the outline of Cameron's muscular body in the other bed. He was asleep. She had suspected he would remain awake most of the night. Her mother often did. Kaleen knew that fey creatures often didn't require much sleep in the mortal realm—or so her mother had always claimed.

But Cameron was asleep. She could make out the rise and fall of his chest. As her eyes adjusted, she realized he wasn't under the covers. He must have just fallen asleep without really planning to do so. That thought brought a faint smile to her lips.

He was so sure of himself. So capable. This made him a little bit more human, though she knew he wasn't, really. Maybe she should have said it made him a little more *real*.

She wanted to know more about him. He intrigued her on every level. She knew he wasn't for her, but why couldn't she at least investigate what it was about him that drew her so strongly? Was that too much to ask?

In the dim hotel room, it didn't seem too much to ask at all. She decided to be bold. Bolder than she had ever been with a man. With anyone, for that matter.

She rolled out of bed as quietly as she could on the far side and got to her feet. She had left the bottle of water on the table. Grabbing that, she sat in the chair and unscrewed the cap on the bottle, taking a swig of water as she put her feet up on the bed. It was time to make her magic work for her.

Invoking a part of her ability that she seldom used, Kaleen closed her eyes and thought about what she wanted. When she reopened her eyes, everything was different. She had invoked the *Sight*. With it, she could see the energy and magic of ordinary things. She could see the way energy flowed from the earth into the trees and plants of her home garden. In this setting, the brightest thing was the man in the bed just across from her.

He glowed with an aura of pure golden energy. Blessed Light that formed into a suit of armor surrounding him in the Goddess's blessing, even as she watched. It was truly amazing. She had never thought to see anything like that in her lifetime, but now, she had no doubts left at all. Cameron was truly a servant of the Goddess. That kind of thing could never be faked or imitated. Especially when he was asleep and didn't even know she had the skill to *See*.

This spoke volumes about the purity and strength of his spirit. Somehow, it made him even more attractive to her. *Darn it.*

She knew there could never be anything between them. Nothing permanent, anyway. She knew she would never live nearly as long as he would. They might be able to have a fling, but that's about all.

Kaleen seriously considered whether or not she could survive heart-whole after having a fling with a man like Cameron. Probably not, she decided. But might it be worth it? She didn't have an answer to that question.

As she sat there contemplating him, she drifted back to sleep.

Cameron didn't know what awakened him, but it was still dark. He looked around the dim room and spotted Kaleen, sitting in the chair, her head resting against the back of it at what had to be an uncomfortable angle. She was asleep, which was odd, because the last thing he had known, she had been asleep in the bed, tucked comfortably under the covers.

The fact that she must've gotten up and moved to the chair troubled him, because that sort of thing should have awakened him. It hadn't. Either she had to be the quietest woman ever born, or for some reason, his subconscious didn't think to alert him to her movements. Perhaps, he saw her as *safe*. Although, that didn't make a lot of sense. He was supposed to be protecting her. To do that, he had to be aware of her movements. The fact that she had gotten up and moved around the room without him knowing was perplexing, to say the least.

As it was, she didn't look very comfortable. He sat up, swinging his legs down to the floor. He sat on the side of the bed for a moment, contemplating her position. She was facing him. Her feet were on the bed, little pink socks covering her dainty toes. An open bottle of water sat beside her on the table. It was half-empty.

He formulated the scenario in his mind. She woke up, got out of bed, retrieved a bottle of water and drank some, sitting in the chair facing him. She had to have been watching him sleep.

But why?

A little thrill shot through him at the idea that she might be as fascinated by him as he was by her. Had she made a study of him? Or had it just been a quirk of the chair facing in his direction? A renegade part of him wanted to believe it was the former. It wanted to think that maybe she might be attracted to him.

But that would never do. Anything between them could only be temporary. She might be part-fey but she was still half-human, despite the dryad blood. He really had no idea how that would affect her longevity or her magic. Cameron, despite his disdain for it, was in line for the throne—albeit far down the line. His family would have something to say about any permanent liaisons.

Sure, he and Kaleen could have a fling, but he wasn't altogether certain that would be enough. There was something about Kaleen that drew him on a much more powerful level. A short-term affair—even if it lasted for decades—would likely never be enough. She made him think about a lifelong commitment which, for his kind, meant eternity.

He'd wanted that before and it had been denied. His parents claimed Molly had just been a folly of youth. They'd disdained the idea that she could have been his true mate—the way shifters had true mates. Fey were different, they'd told him. They didn't always find one special person who was meant just for them.

But Cameron had truly believed Molly had been his One, like the bloodletters talked about. Only...with the perspective of all these centuries without her, he was beginning to think that maybe his parents had been right. Not that he would ever tell them that.

He looked at the mating mark on his forearm and wasn't all that surprised to see it had faded even more. He'd carried it all these years, and now, out of the blue, it was beginning to fade. Just when he'd met a woman who stirred him as no woman had stirred him since his youth.

That thought should've scared the life out of him. He had never encountered anyone since Molly that had made him think about sharing forever with her...and only her.

Kaleen, though he'd only known her a short time, changed all the rules. Everything about her challenged everything he had known to this point. She churned his feelings into a lather and left his senses reeling with attraction and interest. Two things he wasn't really free to explore. At least, not now. Perhaps not ever. He had to get her safely to Wyoming. That's all he should be concentrating on at the moment.

But looking at her awkward position in the chair, he couldn't in good conscience leave her like that. She'd wake up in pain if he let her stay like that much longer. With no other intention than making her more comfortable, he got up and walked quietly over to where she sat.

Cameron put one arm under her knees and the other around her back and lifted her into his arms. It was only a short turn to place her on her bed. The blankets were already pushed back from when she'd gotten up, so he lay her on the sheet, aiming her head for the pillow. He removed his arm from under her knees first, then lowered her toward the pillow while trying to remove his other arm from around her back. That's when he ran into resistance.

He wasn't sure if she was awake or still asleep, but either way, her arms came up to loosely encircle his shoulders. She lifted her head so that their lips were only inches apart. Then centimeters. Then much too close for his comfort...only a whisper apart.

She moved closer, until their lips were touching in a kiss filled with wonder. He knew he shouldn't let it happen, but he was powerless to resist. Her mouth was soft with sleep, her lips plump and moist beneath his. She was temptation itself, and in the darkness of that hotel room, he gave in and allowed himself to kiss her again.

Had it really only been earlier that day when they'd first encountered each other? It felt like he'd known her so much longer. They had shared so much already. And the attraction was undeniable.

He feared she was still asleep and didn't really know what she was doing. The fact that she had initiated this kiss alleviated some of his guilt, but not all of it. Using all his strength of will, he drew back, ending the kiss that he had wanted so desperately.

Cameron looked down at her and realized she was definitely still asleep. Her eyes were closed, and a dreamy expression graced her lovely face. Cameron shook his head and moved away from her after tucking her under the covers once again.

Though it was one of the hardest things he'd ever done, he left her and went back to his side of the room. He couldn't leave her completely. She was still under his care. He was her protector, though he hadn't done a very good job of protecting her from himself just now.

Still, it was only a kiss. A kiss that would linger in his memory for many years to come, he was sure. Her sweet innocence and unconscious allure were altogether out of his experience, and utterly enthralling.

Cameron sat at the desk and, taking a paper and pen from the top drawer, set about making plans for the rest of their trip. Normally, he would use modern technology such as his beloved smartphone, but with the recent uncertainty about the safety of communications, he was taking the precaution of going low-tech. Paper and pen were good enough for the fey realm. They'd be good enough here as well.

Kaleen woke disoriented. The sun was peeking from behind the curtain over the hotel room's only window, and somehow, she was back in bed. She distinctly remembered getting up in the middle of the night and sitting in the chair, but she didn't remember how she got back to bed... Until she did.

Sweet Mother of All. She hadn't dreamed it. She'd kissed Cameron again as he picked her up and put her back in bed. Heat rushed to her cheeks, and she wondered what he would say about it. *Damn*.

She'd been mostly asleep, but she remembered the heat and feel of him against her. His cheek had been bristly with the beard he kept trimmed, and his lips had been warm and hard against hers. He smelled of pine and magic and something like cinnamon. He was warm and hard, his shoulders rippling with muscle in a way that made her mouth go dry with anticipation.

Whoa, girl. She had to get control of herself. They had a long way to go before they reached Wyoming, and she couldn't jump the poor man. He'd put her firmly away from him after their all-too-brief kiss. She remembered that. She'd thought it was just a dream, so she'd sunk back into sleep and kept fantasizing about the man who lit her fuse like nobody's business.

She hoped she hadn't moaned in her sleep or something equally embarrassing. Her cheeks were burning up as heat flooded them. This was definitely one of the most embarrassing situations she'd ever found herself in. Kaleen supposed she'd just have to brazen it out. Maybe she could pretend she didn't remember?

Bluff her way out of it. Sure. That might work. Maybe. If she could keep from blushing every time she looked at him or thought about that tempestuous kiss. *Sheesh.*

"If you're awake, we should think about getting back on the road." Cameron's voice came to her as she lay abed, willing her cheeks to fade back to their normal color.

He was sitting at the desk, writing something. He must have heard her move or something because he hadn't turned his head in the slightest, yet he'd somehow perceived she was awake.

She might as well get up and start getting ready to make a move. They had a long way to go, and the sooner they got on the road, the sooner they would reach their destination. Kaleen swung her legs down and sat on the side of the bed. She wasn't going to mention the fact that he'd put her back in the bed earlier. For now, she was going to studiously ignore what had happened between them. She knew she was taking the coward's way out, but she couldn't help it. It was too early to start tackling these sorts of problems. She had to get her bearings first and wake all the way up. At least, that's what she told herself.

Grabbing her bag, she fled into the bathroom and got ready for the day. She showered and changed into clean clothes, then made sure she repacked all her things. Within about twenty minutes, she was out of the bathroom and doing a final check on her side of the hotel room to make sure she wasn't leaving anything behind.

"We can get breakfast on the road," Cameron said as he retrieved the bag of sandwiches from the mini fridge. They were still good and would make a decent lunch.

"I'd like that. I saw a fast-food place up by the highway entrance. That chain has pretty good egg sandwiches, and I'm pretty sure they had a drive-thru," she contributed.

"Sounds good." He had all the gear he'd brought into the room last night packed up and ready to go.

She did a final check of the area and met him at the door. As she passed him and went out into the hallway, she could have sworn she heard him take a quick breath as if startled. Or perhaps...aroused?

She didn't dare look, but she got the feeling that maybe he hadn't been as dispassionate about their kiss as she'd thought.

Chapter Seven

C ameron didn't bring up the kiss, though it was uppermost in his mind as he watched her scurry around and try to hide her blushes. He wondered if she was mortified because they had kissed for a second time, or because she had allowed it while half-asleep. Maybe he should apologize. Or maybe not.

Best not to mention it for now, he thought, going about the business of getting them back on their road, headed toward their destination. They got breakfast at the drive-thru she'd remembered and ate as they drove, heading ever westward.

Sometime after noon, Cameron spied a simple rest stop that was not much more than a small building that had restrooms and a few vending machines. They had the leftover sandwiches that they really should eat, but a stop wouldn't come amiss, so he pulled off the highway into the rest stop. He stood guard while she used the ladies' room and zipped in to take care of his own comfort as quickly as he could. They tidied up the trash from breakfast and threw it in the trash can, then broke out the sandwiches, plus a few beverages they'd bought from the vending machines. He'd noted the chocolate bars she'd purchased but hadn't said anything.

The rest stop was pretty much empty except for their vehicle. Likewise, there wasn't much traffic on the highway. Cameron was noting the cars that passed, and when he spotted a black SUV go past, then the exact same make and model head back the other direction a few minutes later, his antennae went up. Time to go.

He didn't want to alarm Kaleen, just in case he was being overly cautious, so he kept an eye out as they got back on the road. Sure enough, the black SUV showed up behind them a few minutes later. He cursed under his breath.

"We're being followed," Cameron told Kaleen quietly, his eyes on the rearview mirror.

She nearly jumped, her head whipping around to look at him.

"We are?" She sounded breathless, and not in a good way. He would much rather have heard that tone from passion instead of fear.

He nodded. "Black SUV in the left lane," he said shortly. "We're going to have to stop somewhere out of the way."

"We are?" she repeated herself, this time, her words rising in alarm.

"It's the only way," he told her, shaking his head just once, regretfully. "We can't outrun much of anything in this vehicle for long. We'll need gas soon, for one thing. Also, they can call in reinforcements the farther we travel. If we deal with this here and now, we gain the small advantage of picking the battlefield. It's not much, but we have to work with what we have."

"Trees," she said, after a moment's silence. "If we can find some trees, I'll have a better chance of being able to help."

"Good thinking," he replied, sending her a small grin. "Try not to worry. You're a formidable, little sparrow. And you have me by your side. Together, we can handle just about anything."

Kaleen wished she had his confidence. But she did have one thing he didn't know about yet. She put her hand in her pocket and slipped on the ring her mother had given her. Kaleen had never used it in battle, but she knew it had power, and it might be just the thing to help get them out of this in one piece.

Her mother had sworn her to secrecy and had made Kaleen promise not to use the ring unless there was dire need. Kaleen knew her mother would approve of its use now. Being chased by evil mages—or whoever was in that sinister black car—was definitely a dire situation. If the ring could help, Kaleen knew her mother would be all for Kaleen's first use of it.

By rights, it was her mother's ring and would not be passed down to Kaleen until her mother's death. But her mother had not wanted to bring it back to the fey realm with her, lest it be stolen from her. It was too powerful an artifact to take chances with, and so, Kaleen's mother had left it with its rightful heir for safekeeping. It was also meant to keep Kaleen safe. It was an object of power, and if Kaleen used it correctly, it could protect both her and Cameron.

"There," Cameron said quietly, pulling off the highway.

He took the ramp and then turned quickly onto a small country road that led into a stand of trees. It was a state park, Kaleen saw, as they passed a tall wooden sign. This was some sort of back entrance to the trailhead of a few hiking trails. There was a small gravel parking lot that was, thankfully, empty. And trees all around.

"How about this?" Cameron asked as he parked the car in the far corner of the lot, closest to the trees.

"Perfect," she told him, already getting out of the car and heading for the trees.

They were welcoming to her, pleased with the taste of her power. She tried to communicate with them, letting them know that trouble was coming, but she had barely made her explanation—not communicating in words, but rather images and feelings—when the dreaded black SUV pulled into view.

"Get into the trees and stay there. I'll handle this," Cameron said, not sounding the least bit fearful. He was a brave man, that was for certain, but she didn't enjoy being a damsel in distress.

"I can help you," she told him, her tone insistent.

He turned to look at her as the SUV rolled to a stop ten yards away, and a woman got out of the passenger side. She was followed by the man who'd been driving. Both were forming evil-looking balls of power in their open palms in preparation for lobbing them at Cameron and Kaleen.

"Friends," Cameron called out to the newcomers, facing them with a facetious grin on his face. "Can't we settle this without fighting?"

"We came for the girl, but you're too tasty to pass up," the woman said, licking her lips in a sickening way as she ogled Cameron.

"And to answer your question, no. We cannot leave without your power. The *Mater Priori* demands more power, and we need to collect all we can to please her," the man answered.

"What happens if you fail?" Cameron asked, sounding truly interested.

"Then she dines on our power," the man replied. "So, you see, we cannot afford to fail."

"Tell me this one thing first, though," Cameron said in a light tone. "Have you seen Elspeth with your own eyes?" He made it sound like something he wanted to do, but Kaleen realized belatedly that he was pumping these people for information.

"We have," the woman answered, "and she is glorious."

"But she needs you to kill for her so she can regain her strength," Cameron sounded as if he were only considering an interesting fact rather than the murder of innocents to feed the evil of the Destroyer. Kaleen was appalled, but she had faith in Cameron. He was playing them.

"I would do anything for her," the man said, sounding more and more like some kind of cultist. Kaleen figured that's what the followers of Elspeth amounted to, more or less.

"Then she is nearby," Cameron pushed for even more information.

That's when the male let loose with the energy ball he'd been forming. It was a sickly green. Not the green of the earth and growing things, but the green of illness and pestilence. Kaleen wanted to gag as the oily energy rolled off Cameron's shield, which he'd placed around Kaleen as well as himself.

"We cannot tell you where she is, though you will meet her soon, through us. You won't know it, but your power will go straight to her, to fuel her great cause," the woman said, her energy a sulfurous yellow.

"I'd rather not," Kaleen said, feeling annoyed more than scared by these two idiots. Oh, she wasn't underestimating them. Their power certainly seemed formidable, but she wasn't going to cower in fear. Especially not when she was wearing her mother's ring.

It pulsed on her finger, wanting a chance to do its thing. The ring hadn't been used in years, and it had a lot of pent-up power ready to be let loose at Kaleen's merest thought. It was like trying to hold back an eager stallion, but she had to make it accede to her will. She would master the ring, not have the ring master her. That was one of her mother's most important lessons about being a ring bearer, and Kaleen would not fail at the first test.

"You have no choice in the matter," the woman screamed, completely unhinged as she let loose a barrage of yellow vapor at them.

Cameron's shield would have held, but it was time for Kaleen to be an equal partner in this endeavor. She hadn't been ready before, but this time, she was not caught unprepared. After what had happened to her beloved garden, she vowed never to be taken by surprise like that again for as long as she lived.

Kaleen held up her hand, palm outward, the ring pulsing the energy back at the two mages, making them stagger and fall on their backsides in the dusty gravel. They got to their feet and redoubled their efforts. She repulsed them again, sending their own energy back against them. This time, they stayed down longer.

"Stop this," Kaleen ordered in her best command voice, but the mages didn't listen. They were being driven on by something she didn't fully understand.

They came against her a third time, and this time, it was a killing blow. Their own magic struck them both down, never to rise again.

Cameron looked at her with wonder and suspicion in his eyes. "You're going to tell me how you did that once we're back on the road," he said, already moving toward the downed mages. She followed at a slower pace, afraid of what she might find.

But she needn't have worried. The only thing left of them was two piles of ashy clothing. Their bodies had been completely incinerated by their own magic. Nasty.

Cameron looked for a wallet in the man's pockets while Kaleen picked up the woman's purse. There was a shock spell on the bag, but the ring negated it without harm. In fact, now that Kaleen was wearing the ring, she could tell that the bag held no further nastiness, just the trappings of a modern woman's life, including her cellphone, wallet, credit cards, makeup and other bits of her life.

It was sad, really. Kaleen hadn't even known the woman's name. She opened the wallet and looked at the woman's driver's license.

"Paula Rillion," Kaleen said, reading from the little card as Cameron opened the man's wallet.

"Chester Rillion," he said, his deep voice echoing with the same sentiment she was feeling. What a waste of two lives, but they'd chosen evil, and this was just the harvest of what they had sown.

"Husband and wife or brother and sister?" Kaleen wondered.

"No rings," Cameron mused, looking at the remains more closely. "It's not conclusive, but I'd say siblings, not mates." He shook his head again. "Go back to the car while I tidy this up. I'll ask the shifters to send somebody for the SUV once we get where we're going. Chances are nobody will notice if it's parked here for a few hours."

Saddened by what she had done, Kaleen knew it had been necessary. Still, she was glad Cameron was there and thinking clearly. She went back to their vehicle while he picked up the clothes and shook them out, folding them neatly and putting them into the back of SUV, behind the front seats. He conducted a quick search of the vehicle, then got in and parked it out of the way in the back corner of the lot.

He got out of the black SUV, then hopped into their vehicle and started it up. They were on their way in short order, rejoining the highway and heading west once more. They were quiet for a number of miles, and then, Cameron turned to look at her, splitting his attention between Kaleen and the road.

"Do you want to tell me how you did that?" His tone was slightly challenging, but Kaleen understood how he must be feeling.

She'd been inept and out of her league yesterday in the garden, and then, suddenly today, she was a freaking sorceress? It didn't add up. Unless you factored in the ring.

She moved her hand in front of him. "I finally put this on. It is my mother's. She left it here to keep it safe from her family and also to keep me safe, should I come into danger."

Cameron looked justifiably taken aback. She brought her hand back to her side of the car and studied the pretty bauble that held so much power.

"I didn't know you had one of the rings of power," Cameron said with quiet respect as he drove along.

She held her hand up to the sunlight and marveled at the gleam of the metal and sparkle of the faceted stone at the ring's heart. It was very pretty and deceptively fragile looking for something that contained so much power.

"*Three rings for elven kings under the sky,*" she quoted from the famous fantasy trilogy by a long-dead Oxford don.

"Tolkein must have had dealings with our folk. He knew about the rings. I wonder if he made up the rest of it?" Cameron observed.

"Beats me. My mother left this with me for safekeeping, but I don't really know much about its history or lore. What do you know of the rings?" she asked Cameron, turning to look at him.

"Only those born to royal lineages may use the rings of power," Cameron told her. "Therefore, you must be a princess, or the like."

She laughed. "I'm a mongrel half-fey. Not welcome in the realm of my mother's birth at all, according to her. She chose to live here to be with my father, but her family was enraged. So much so, that they kidnapped him as punishment and in order to entice her back. She refused to put me in danger from her family, especially when I was just a child, so she stayed here until I was eighteen and could fend for myself legally. But she left her ring with me because she didn't want her family to have it. She is the heir. The ring belongs to her line. Therefore, it would be mine after her passing. They wanted to give it to her brother, but he was the one who encouraged her to leave and made it possible for her to travel Between. He loves her. He wants her to be happy. But their guardian had other ideas."

Chapter Eight

T hat told Cameron quite a bit. He was almost certain he knew who her grandparents had been. They were long gone, and a guardian—an uncle, he thought—had raised Kaleen's mother and her little brother. As eldest, she was the heir to the lands and title. Kaleen's mother had to be the Duchess of Eriwande. Heir to one of the proud noble lineages.

He thought he remembered hearing that she had a younger brother, and an older relation—and uncle, he recalled—had stepped in to raise them when both of their parents had died. The younger brother now captained the armies of Eriwande, while the uncle had stepped in to fulfill whatever obligations the family had to the High Court. Cameron had met the brother a few times and thought him an able warrior, as well as a fair and noble man. Cameron hadn't really wanted much to do with the High Court and didn't know the uncle. As a younger son, Cameron preferred to live his own life. That had been especially true since becoming a Knight. He had a higher calling than merely being a spare son to the fey realm's monarch.

"You are by no means a mongrel," Cameron said with a growl. "Don't ever refer to yourself that way."

She looked at him with surprise. "Mother said that all fey would disdain me because of my birth."

"Not all, milady. I'm sorry that your mother had such a bad experience with those around her, but we are not all bigots against humanity. I, myself, have an aunt who chooses to live in the mortal realm, though she visits the High Court every once in a long while. As you may know, travelling Between isn't always easy or predictable. She says she prefers this realm to all others and the people here to almost everyone back in the fey realm."

"Hm." She seemed to think about that for a moment. "Well then. I stand corrected. But Mother was rather adamant that I would not be accepted or welcomed among her family, and I believe that."

"No reason to doubt your mother's words. I just want you to know that not all fey feel that way. I would not have devoted so much of my life to helping here in mortal realm with the battle against Elspeth if that were the case," he pointed out. "I rather like humans, though it's heartbreaking when a friend dies."

Should he tell her about Molly? No. Not yet. Maybe not ever. He couldn't bring himself to talk about Molly to anyone. Not in any depth. He decided to shift the conversation to something a little brighter, if he could.

"The shifters live longer and are a lot of fun to be around," he went on. "Shifters really know how to party, if you'll pardon the expression. But you'll soon learn the truth of it when we get to Pack lands. Sally and Maria have mated into a very strong wolf Pack, and I'm sure they'll welcome you as happily as they've welcomed the other part-dryads they've already found. Packs are all about family, and you are part of theirs now, through your distant cousins."

She seemed to think about that for a moment. "That's going to take some getting used to, if I'm honest," she said finally.

"Don't be surprised at how easily those shifters win you over. Wolves are kind of adorable in a fierce sort of way, but don't ever tell them I said that." He winked at her as she looked shocked and then smiled. "If we keep making good time, we should be there sometime tonight. We were lucky with the good weather and little traffic."

"So soon?"

Was Cameron reading a hint of regret into her words, or was that simply fear of the next part of her journey toward meeting her extended family? He couldn't be sure. Maybe she felt as he did about their time alone coming to an end.

"It'll be after dinner, but before midnight, I think. If all goes as planned," he told her. At least they'd have one more meal alone together. It would probably be fast food, but the company mattered more than the food to him right now.

"They won't mind us arriving so late?"

"Not at all. Wolves tend to run a lot at night, so someone will definitely be up at the Pack house to receive us. Shifters—and most magical races, for that matter—usually don't require as much sleep as non-magical humans. The magic sustains them, and shifters, in general, tend to spend the hours of darkness in their furry forms, when regular folk are asleep, and the world is more like it was before the age of man and machines."

She nodded, thinking about that for a long moment, then the conversation turned to what they would have for dinner. Cameron's own prediction came true a few hours later when they got burgers from a rest stop on the side of the highway. They stopped for just a few minutes to eat and stretch, then got back on the road. They were so close now, he was eager to deliver Kaleen safely to her family, even if it did mean the end of his time alone with her. Perhaps that was for the best.

Around nine o'clock at night, they rolled up the driveway of the Pack house. Cameron hadn't called ahead. The communications were still on lockdown, and he didn't want to give the enemy any detailed information about Kaleen's location or expected time of arrival.

Cameron could see Sally peering out the front window of the dining hall, and Jason opened the front door to check out who had just arrived. It was clear the Alpha couple had been waiting for Kaleen's arrival, but she sat in the passenger seat for a moment, staring straight ahead, her expression tight.

"What if they don't like me?" she whispered, and Cameron realized she was nervous.

He reached out to put his hand over hers. "They're going to love you," he told her, trying to reassure her. "You're a very loveable person," he went on, trying to make her smile.

She turned her head to meet his gaze, and he wanted so much to lean over and kiss her, but he resisted. It was one of the hardest things he'd ever had to do, but it was for the best.

"Thanks for everything you've done to help me," she said, her voice soft in the quiet interior of the car. "I owe you one." The ghost of a smile slipped across her features.

"As I recall, we're probably about even, but I appreciate your meaning." Their eyes met and held, as if she was just as reticent as he about their time together ending. He caught movement out of the corner of his eye, and the moment was broken. "Don't look now, but Sally's on her way out. She's taken to being the Alpha female of this Pack like the proverbial duck to water, despite the fact that she can't shift. She's a strong spirit, but I think you two will hit it off."

"I hope you're right." A bit of her nervousness returned, but Kaleen put her hand out to open the door on her side of the car. Cameron took that as his cue to get out and offer assistance, if needed.

He came around to her side of the car and helped with her door as Sally approached with Jason following close behind. Kaleen slid out of the vehicle, and Cameron stepped back so the distant cousins could see each other. Cameron met Jason's gaze, and the two men nodded to each other as the women faced each other. Cameron made the introductions.

"Kaleen, this is Sally Moore and her mate, Jason, the Alpha pair of this Pack. Sally, this is your cousin, Kaleen." It wasn't very formal, but it covered the necessities. Introductions in the fey realm could go on for much longer, especially in the High Court, but Cameron didn't like all that folderol. The mortal realm was a lot simpler, sometimes.

"I'm so glad you're here," Sally said, taking Kaleen's offered hand and smiling. "I've put out the word, and the rest of our cousins and my sister are going to be arriving shortly."

Cameron was impressed. That was fast work. Then again, there was no time to waste now that the enemy knew of their plans.

Sally turned and ushered Kaleen toward the Pack house. Jason held back, standing next to Cameron. They walked more slowly toward the house, following in the women's wake.

"Most of the others are flying in," Jason told him. "We'll be doing fast runs from the airstrip to here tonight and tomorrow. Jesse's coordinating protection, but I thought I'd ask if you wouldn't mind helping. It would be a shame to lose one of the seven now to carelessness. Sally has worked so hard to find them, and she's so happy to have family. It would break her heart to lose any of them."

"I can see that, Alpha. I would be glad to assist in whatever way I can. You should know, though, that Kaleen holds a very powerful and protective magical artifact. If anything crops up, she can help defend your lady and the others quite well." Cameron knew it was only fair to warn the Alpha. He wouldn't tell tales, but he needed to know what was in his territory so he could make use of all their assets.

"You don't say?" Jason had a more contemplative look on his face than Cameron had expected. "Between you and I, there has been a resurgence in the appearance of magical artifacts lately—both good and bad. I don't think that's a very good sign. What is it Kaleen bears, if I may ask?"

"Nothing of this realm. It is a family heirloom from her fey ancestors. An object of great power that will answer only to one of her direct family line."

The rings could change allegiance, he'd heard, but the Alpha didn't need to know that. Even in the fey realm, that knowledge was a closely held secret known only to those who were in line to inherit. It was a warning given to youngsters of those lofty houses that if they didn't straighten up and behave correctly, the ring could bypass them in favor of another. Only those of strong moral character could bear such a burden. Only those with a pure heart could wield it as Kaleen had done.

"Fey magic," Jason observed, watching the women enter the house. Then, he sighed. "I suppose we need all the help we can get if we're going to do this thing."

"Aye, my friend. That we do."

Kaleen was nervous to meet Sally in person, but she needn't have worried. Sally was a doll and so very welcoming. The Pack house was really nice, and Kaleen was nearly overwhelmed by how nice everybody was to her. They made her feel welcome at every turn, from the older ladies knitting in one corner to the little ragamuffins running around playing while their parents supervised.

It was after dinner, but Sally offered her coffee and a selection of desserts as they sat in the communal dining room. Kaleen looked around to find Cameron. He was just entering with Jason, and her eyes met his across the space. He nodded encouragingly, and she felt...somehow...safer with him present. She'd become very attached to him over the past couple of days and didn't like it when they were separated, even for a short time.

She wondered if that would continue, or if it was just a temporary effect. Time would tell. For now, she had to gear up for meeting more of her newly discovered extended family.

"Ah, here's Maria and Jesse," Sally said, turning toward the archway, where a handsome couple was just arriving. The woman made a beeline for their table while the man followed more slowly, detouring to exchange greetings with Cameron and Jason.

Maria was just as nice and even more outgoing than Sally. She was softer, in some ways, her caring nature showing her in kind eyes. Sally had been a detective, Kaleen knew, and Maria was a veterinarian. Cameron had told her a lot about the people she would be meeting as they drove along, and she felt she knew them already.

"Arlo is on his way down the mountain with Pam," Maria told them once they'd exchanged greetings. "Some of the others will be arriving later tonight, but I'm not sure who or when. The guys are keeping all communication very limited because of the leak, or whatever it really is. I can't believe anyone in the Pack would betray anything."

"Sunny and Dennis were visiting Crystal and Marco in Nebraska, so they'll all be traveling here together. They'll be arriving sometime later tonight," Sally told them. "I'm hoping Cece and Deke will show up tomorrow. The sooner we can do the spell, the better."

There was a small commotion at the entrance to the dining hall and a woman came into the room. Kaleen stood, recognizing something about the newcomer immediately. This had to be her cousin. Her *first* cousin. The daughter of her father's sister. She would know her anywhere.

"You're Pamela," Kaleen said as the other woman stopped right in front of her.

"And you're Kaleen," the woman replied, nodding. They stood in silence for a moment, then Pam smiled. "You have no idea how happy I am to meet you."

Kaleen returned the smile. "Me too. I didn't even know my father had a sister until Cameron told me, but you look so familiar. You have my father's eyes."

"And you have my mother's nose," Pam added, staring at Kaleen's face with wistful eyes. "There's a definite family resemblance."

"There is," Sally agreed, coming up to stand at their side, looking from Pam to Kaleen and back again. "You two could be sisters, not just first cousins. Except for the coloring."

"My mother is fey," Kaleen said, fingering her own long blonde hair. "I got the blonde from her."

Pam was nodding. "No fey in my family. Just Mom's dryad side. My dad was just a regular guy with no magic as far as I know."

Kaleen reached out to Pam, touching her arm. "Cameron told me a little of your background. I'm very sorry to hear of your losses. My parents have been gone a long time, but I have hope they survive in the fey realm."

"For your sake, I hope they survive too," Pam offered kindly. "And thanks for your sympathy. I lost them a long time ago, but it still hurts sometimes, to think about it."

Kaleen couldn't hold back. She stepped forward and hugged her cousin, patting her back gently. "I know," she commiserated. "It gets lonely making your way all by yourself in this world." Kaleen stepped back after a moment, and both of them had shining eyes from the unexpressed emotion that rode them. "But I hear you're mated now," Kaleen said with a bright smile, turning to happier thoughts.

"I am," Pam agreed, looking back over her shoulder to the man who stood not too far away, watching them. She held out her hand, and he came right over, taking her fingers in his. "Kaleen, this is my mate, Arlo Makepeace."

"I'm pleased to meet you, cousin-in-law," Kaleen joked. Arlo had a friendly smile and striking good looks. He shook her hand and seemed genuinely glad to make her acquaintance.

"Good to know you," he said quietly, in his deep voice. "Pam's talked about nothing else but meeting you since we found out you were on your way. I'm glad you made it to us safely."

"That's Cameron's doing," Kaleen admitted freely. "I didn't think there was any danger, but I was very wrong, and Cameron helped me out of a tight spot when goons attacked in my own back garden." She frowned, thinking of the destruction. "We had to leave the garden in a huge mess."

"Oh, that's tough," Pam said. "Maybe when this is all over, I can help you fix it back up."

It was kind of her to offer, but Kaleen wasn't sure it would be safe to go back home anytime soon. Pam must have known that, as well.

"When it's safe again, I'd love to have you come visit," Kaleen said politely, hoping that, someday, her invitation might be fulfilled.

"Well, that's why we're all here," Pam replied, looking around at the other dryad descendants and nodding to Sally, who still stood nearby. "What can I do to help?"

Arlo excused himself to go talk to some friends of his, and Pam joined the rest of the ladies at the table. They picked up their discussion as Pam sat next to Kaleen.

"We'll need to do some prep work before we can attempt the Elven Star," Kaleen said as the planning resumed in earnest. "I can help with that, and I'm sure Cameron will tell us exactly what we should do. After all, this spell is of the fey realm. It's not something done here often, and if we get it right, it's going to unleash a heck of a lot of power. We need to have things ready to funnel the extra power into something useful like better shields for your Pack."

Both women looked at her in surprise. "We can do that?" Sally asked.

"I don't see why not," Kaleen told her. "I'm no expert, but my mother did teach me everything she could before she left. I believe we could produce some very neat wards with the leftover energy when we dissipate the Elven Star. It's protective magic, that much I know. Instead of just earthing it and letting all that effort flow away, we could channel it into something that would protect this forest and the people living in it for centuries to come."

"You're talking about a permanent ward?" Sally said, looking impressed.

Kaleen was impressed that Sally knew about permanent wards at all. They weren't something most non-mages knew about, and the specific kind of talent required to cast them was very rare indeed.

"Yes, or something very close. Mother said only very special mages could cast permanent wards by themselves. This would be more of a collective effort, but it would have essentially the same effect," Kaleen replied, enthused. "We should ask Cameron when he has a moment. As I said, he knows a great deal more about fey spell work than I do. I'm only half-fey."

"That's more than either of us," Maria said with a grin, pointing between Sally and herself.

"This is great, Kaleen," Sally said, nodding with contentment. "We could really use some extra protection around Pack lands. We've already had one direct attack on Leonora's tree. The enemy knows where we are and clearly see us as a threat. If we can provide more protection for our land and people, I'm all for it, and I know Jason will be as well."

"Then we'll talk with Cameron and make some plans. I don't sleep as much as regular people, so I can start on preparations tonight. I'm pretty sure we'll need to gather a few things before we can attempt the spell, both to achieve our main objective of freeing Leonora and healing her, and the secondary plan to channel the residual power into wards for your Pack's territory." Kaleen thought about that. "I think I'll need to see a map or something that gives me a better idea of the terrain we'll want to ward."

Sally stood, and the two other women followed suit. "Jason's got a map in the back office here. Come on, I'll show you."

Kaleen followed Sally out of the dining room and down a large hallway and then a smaller one toward the back of the house. She cast her glance back at Cameron, standing with the other men in the larger hall just outside the dining room's arched entrance. He was watching her, his gaze making her blood heat with attraction.

He really was the most attractive man she'd ever met. It wasn't just his stature, warrior's build or good looks. It was his character and calling. His humor and wit. His good nature and loyalty to the cause of good to which he had sworn an oath. Even next to those handsome shifters, he was more appealing to her in every way that counted. *Darn it*. He was fey. He wouldn't stay in the mortal realm, and he would outlive her. Getting involved in any way with him would only lead to heartache. She had to be sensible about this, but her heart was saying something completely different. Silly heart.

Chapter Nine

C ameron watched Kaleen leave the dining room with the other ladies and head for the back office. He wondered what they were up to, but he had tasks of his own to complete. He'd asked the Alphas to intervene with any local shifter groups near where they'd had the run-in with the mages to remove the vehicle and make sure no trace was left. Jason had taken care of that with a quick phone call, much to Cameron's relief. And Jesse was updating him on the status of the search for the source of their information leak.

"So far, we've been able to eliminate all the computer systems farther up the mountain in the Wraith compound, but the Pack house is still questionable. We've gotten new phones for all the leadership. They went live this afternoon, but it's not like upgrading existing phones. We can't let all the apps and contact information carry over in case the bug—or whatever it is—comes over with that. So, it's a case of manually setting up the new phones by punching in numbers and downloading only a very few approved apps to start until we can be sure where the leak originated. Our network has been checked, but there are still one or two trouble spots that we haven't been able to clear yet. The most concerning is Jason's office here at the Pack house. The computer in there is not coming up clean, and the tech isn't sure if it's just because the system is dirty from people sneaking in there and searching the net or if someone's tampered with it from the outside. Either way, the safest thing would be to replace the whole system, but that's going to take another day, at least." Jesse frowned. "In the meantime, we're not using the office, just in case."

"But the women just went back that way," Cameron pointed out as Jason and Jesse both frowned.

"Surely not," Jesse said, already on the move. Cameron and Jason followed quickly behind. "I told Maria—"

He didn't finish that sentence, but Cameron got the gist. The three of them went down the narrower back hallway and right to the office. Sure enough, the women were all there, standing over the desk, staring down at a map.

"Ladies," Jesse began, moving directly to his mate, Maria, "I thought I told you that the office hasn't been cleared." He was talking to Maria, moderating his tone as he touched her shoulder with concern. This was a new side to Jesse—the cold-as-ice warrior who was hell on wheels in the field—that Cameron had never quite seen before.

"I thought that only meant the computer. We're not using that. Just looking at maps."

"Why are you looking at maps?" Jason asked, moving to stand behind his mate, Sally. He was looking over her shoulder at the map.

Suddenly, Cameron felt a shiver go down his spine. He'd learned never to ignore such premonitions. He thought they were sent by the Goddess, though he wasn't altogether certain. Still, they were worth heeding. Every time he'd felt one in the past, it had turned out to be a real warning of danger.

"Perhaps we can talk about this outside?" Cameron suggested, meeting everyone's gazes one by one to impress upon them a sense of urgency.

Jesse caught on immediately, his brother Jason, a split-second later. They squeezed their mates' shoulders, and the ladies looked at their mates and then subsided. Cameron strode forward to take the map they'd been studying. He shot Jason a questioning look, and at the Alpha's nod, Cameron rolled up that map and took it with him as they went out of the office.

Cameron closed the door firmly behind himself as he exited the room last. Kaleen was waiting for him just outside the door while the other two couples went to the end of the hall and waited there.

"What is it?" she asked in a low voice. He had no doubt the werewolf brothers at the end of the hall could hear, but they were being discreet.

"I got a tingle. Something's not right in that room," he told her, shaking his head. "I can't be more specific than that right now, but it's not safe to talk in there. I hope you weren't discussing anything too specific with the ladies."

"Not really," she said as they walked down the hall toward the others. "We were just looking at the map. We'd talked about the other stuff in the dining room and then came here so I could see the extent of their territory and the terrain. Sally was just pointing out things like that on the map for me."

"Why?" Cameron asked as they rejoined the others. Jason was looking at them with great interest.

"I'd like to know the answer to that as well," the Alpha said, his tone a bit stern. Cameron supposed he had a right. This was his Pack and his territory. He should be in on any plans they were making regarding both.

"Let's go back into the dining room," Sally suggested, shooing her husband in that direction.

"Is it safe to talk in there?" Kaleen asked Cameron as they followed the others into the larger hallway and then into the dining room.

"I believe so. I didn't get any bad feelings from any other place I've been in this house, but I'll keep my eyes and senses open," Cameron replied as they sat at a big round table near the front window. He didn't sense anything in this room. So far, only the office had given him that shiver of something not quite right.

When they were all seated, Jason spoke first. "What exactly were you ladies up to?"

"Well, Kaleen was telling us about all the extra magical energy that will be summoned when we do the Elven Star spell and how we could redirect it after we're done freeing and healing Leonora, into wards around our Pack lands. That's why she wanted to see a map of the area."

"Wards?" Now, Jason looked intrigued. "How strong would they be? What kind of coverage are we talking about?"

Cameron unrolled the map and laid it out on the table, already warming to the idea of using the excess energy in just such a way. He hadn't given it much thought but was glad it had occurred to Kaleen. Her mother must have taught her a lot more than he'd realized.

"With the amount of magical energy generated by such a spell, we might be able to channel the residue into permanent wards," Cameron said, eyeing the map, looking for the boundaries where they could set the wards.

"You're kidding," Jason commented, his tone filled with disbelief.

"Not kidding," Kaleen said, moving to point out spots on the map to Cameron that she'd already thought of for ward placement. "There are some really good spots here, and they would keep anyone with bad intent from trespassing on Pack lands ever again."

"Seriously?" It was Jesse's turn to be surprised. "That would be amazing, if you can do it."

"I think we can," Kaleen replied, looking up at the Alpha. "At the very least, we can try. We're going to be generating a heck of a lot of magical power when we do this spell, and all of that has to go somewhere when we're done. Normally, if we can't hold it, we'll just earth it. Send it back into the earth. But if we can hold on and direct it, we can put it to good use protecting your land and people."

"That's…" Jason seemed stunned a bit. "That's very kind of you to think of it, and if you ladies can manage it, the Pack, and I, will be extremely grateful. One of the things that has shaken us is how the enemy managed to sneak onto our lands, right under our noses, and go after Leonora's tree directly. That should not have been possible with all of us watching so closely."

"Sally mentioned it, which is why I thought about the wards and how we might be able to help," Kaleen admitted.

They talked about the possibilities for placing the wards, using the map for reference. Once they had come up with a feasible plan, the meeting started to break up. Jesse leaned over to speak to Cameron.

"What was it about the office?" Jesse hadn't forgotten to follow up, he'd just been biding his time.

"I honestly don't know, but something is very wrong in there," Cameron replied.

"We've had the techs check every inch of this building, including that office, over and over," Jason said, joining the conversation. "I can't even imagine they would've missed anything."

"Trust me," Cameron told them with a sigh, "they did miss something. Don't work or talk in there until somebody figures out what's going on."

"You can't be any more specific than that?" Jesse's eyes narrowed.

Cameron shook his head. "Sorry. I just got a sense of alarm when I was in there. It's nothing I can pinpoint. Wish I could."

"Could it be something magical?" Jason asked.

Cameron tilted his head, considering. "Possibly, but I would bet more on something technological. Perhaps enhanced, or somehow mixed, with magic. If you want, I'll help search the room with one of your electronics experts. I don't have any skill in that area, but perhaps together, we might be able to figure out what it was that set my senses tingling."

"I'll take you up on that," Jason said immediately. "Jesse, can you get one the specialist guys down here?"

Jesse was already reaching for his phone. "I'll call." He looked up at Cameron. "I assume you're willing to do this tonight, right?"

Cameron nodded. "I'm at your disposal."

He wasn't really that tired yet. His kind didn't need much sleep in the first place, though they had been on the road all day, not to mention the excitement they'd faced in that remote parking lot. Still, if the Alpha's office was bugged in some way, that was a high priority item to fix.

"It is getting kind of late," Maria said as Jesse moved off to make his phone call. "How about we show you two your rooms while they wait for the specialist to come down the mountain?"

"Sounds like a good idea," Cameron replied. Even if he wasn't tired, he was pretty sure Kaleen would need to rest soon. He'd feel better if he knew where she was meant to stay in this big house and where he would be able to find her should he seek her out later.

He didn't look too closely at why that mattered to him so much.

Kaleen followed Sally up the stairs and to the left. Cameron was at her side. She was a little surprised when Sally led them to the end of the corridor and a single door that led to a sitting room. Off of that were two more doors taking up the back portion of what had to be a suite.

"There are two bedrooms that share a bath in the middle. I figured you two would like the privacy down this end of the corridor. We have a number of families staying here right now as their houses are being repaired. We had a lot of damage from a wind storm a few weeks ago that's just now being fixed. It was easier to move the families here in the interim, and it's always good for the Pack to have the children around." Sally smiled fondly. "Anyway, this side of the house is quieter, and since you're not wolves, I thought you would be more comfortable sharing this suite. The only single rooms we have are in the bachelor section, and there are a lot of werewolf guys living down there right now. They're kind of loud and partially nocturnal so, all in all, I thought you two would be happier up here."

"It's fine," Kaleen said. "Really. You've been very thoughtful. And the suite is lovely."

She noticed her bags had already been brought up and put in the right-hand bedroom. The door to which was open, and the bedside lamp was on, shedding a rosy glow over the peach-colored bedspread. The other bedroom was blue and green and had a similar setup.

The sitting room had a large television and sectional couch, as well as a good-sized table in one corner. Sally went over to a small closet and opened it.

"There's a coffeemaker and some snacks. Also, a small fridge, if you want to bring up anything from the kitchen and keep it cold for later. I asked them to put a cheese platter in here, in case you get hungry later," she said. "And some cold drinks."

Kaleen could see a selection of juice bottles, as well a few sodas and even a couple of beer bottles. They really had thought of everything. She was amazed by the hospitality of these werewolves.

"That's really nice of you," Kaleen told Sally. "Please pass along my thanks to whoever did all this. It's incredibly thoughtful."

"No problem at all, and I will definitely pass along your gratitude. The ladies who keep the rooms stocked and the kitchen full of delicious food are our maternal wolves. They really run the whole Pack's social structure, though they don't say so out loud. My mate is the Alpha, but he's more in charge of the Pack's security—both day-to-day and into the future—in all senses of that word. He runs the business side of the Pack and keeps order while the maternals run everyone's lives." She laughed at her own statement. "Don't ever tell one of them I said that, though."

Kaleen mimed zipping her lips. "Mum's the word."

Sally winked conspiratorially and left, closing the door to the suite behind herself.

Kaleen turned to Cameron and tried not to feel too awkward. They'd spent a lot of time together over the past days, but this was different somehow.

"I'm going to take a shower and relax," Kaleen announced. "I'm not used to so much travel."

"I'm going back downstairs to figure out the problem in that office," Cameron said quickly. "I don't think it's going to be easily solved, so don't expect me back too soon." His expression tightened. "What I mean to say is that I'll be a while, so take your time and relax. I'll try not to make too much noise when I come back."

He left quickly without giving her a chance to respond. She watched him go with mixed emotions. They'd been so easy with each other to this point. Why was it getting weird all of a sudden?

Chapter Ten

When Cameron got back downstairs, the electronics expert was just coming in the front door. Shifter, Cameron knew right off, but not a wolf. The tall blond man was definitely military, but more...exotic, somehow.

"Ah, good. You're both here," Jesse said as he walked into the front hall from the dining room. "Liam, this is Cameron le Fey. Cameron, this is Liam Kinkaid. He's on loan to us from the Navy for a few days."

"That explains it," Cameron said, reaching out to shake hands with the newcomer. "I've met some of your kin. At least, I assume you're one of the Kinkaid Clan."

The blond man smiled as he shook Cameron's hand. "That I am. Lester's son, if you know some of the elders."

"Indeed, I do. I met Lester once, but mostly, I've dealt with Sam when the need arose and our paths crossed," Cameron explained.

They exchanged a few more pleasantries as they walked down the hallway. As they approached the office door, they got to the heart of the matter.

"I've checked this office three times," Liam said, his tone wary but open. "I have to tell you, my equipment found nothing." Liam had a small briefcase in one hand, and Cameron assumed whatever electronic equipment he was talking about was in there.

"Humor me," Cameron said, putting his hand on the doorknob. "There is something in there, but the more I think about it, the more I come to believe it is some odd mix of magic and technology. I think it will take both of us, working in concert to unmask it." Cameron looked at Jason. "I propose to do a spell of revelation, and while it's in effect, I'd like Liam to use his devices and check the room again. With your permission, Alpha."

Jason nodded slowly. "You have my permission to proceed," he responded formally.

"Thank you, Alpha." Cameron turned back to Liam. "You will need to work fast because I cannot keep the spell up indefinitely."

Liam nodded and turned to the side table just outside the door. He propped his small case on the table and opened up the case, taking out two small black boxes. He placed one in his pocket and raised a small antenna on the other.

"Ready when you are," Liam said, all business now.

Cameron nodded and turned the knob, opening the door. He prepared himself before stepping across the threshold. The moment he did, he invoked the spell, raising his hands and painting a powerful magical glyph in the air with his fingers. He held it and nodded to Liam, who entered the room behind him. Jesse and Jason stayed just outside the open door, watching with great interest as Cameron moved to the center of the room.

Liam started scanning, and Cameron moved the glyph around as Liam moved, keeping it with his area of scan. They were about three quarters of the way through the room when Liam's instrument beeped urgently. Liam frowned, but Cameron felt a moment of satisfaction. He *had* sensed something that the scanner alone could not find.

Liam pulled the smaller box out of his pocket and switched to using that one. Apparently, that was a finer detector that allowed him to zero in on the location of the problem.

It took a few minutes, but he eventually found something on the side of a cardboard box. He lifted things out of the box—reams of blank copy paper, Cameron thought it was—and then turned the box on its side. There was printing on the box. It was an elaborate design with bands of color and thick black lines. In one part of the design, something made the small box in Liam's hand flash an angry red.

Liam nodded at the men, saying nothing, and held up one finger, then indicated they should continue the search. They'd found one device. There could be more.

Cameron held the glyph of revelation while Liam picked up the first detector and began searching again from where they'd left off. He found two more devices, each embedded in the same brand of copy paper boxes, stowed under a table on which sat both a standard photocopier and a laser printer that also functioned as a fax machine and scanner. Well, it was an office, after all. They probably used all that equipment every day, and they needed a supply of paper.

Liam lifted the two full boxes of paper and handed them off to Jesse, who took them somewhere. The first empty box, Liam handed to Jason, but the Alpha didn't leave, just held the box behind himself while he watched Liam and Cameron finish their search of the room. Liam was very thorough, scanning everything, including the ceiling and the floor, but the paper boxes were the only things found.

Liam nodded to Cameron when he was done, and Cameron let the glyph go with a weary sigh. It wasn't hugely taxing, but it did require effort to hold the glyph, so he was just as happy they were done with that task. They couldn't talk freely until the boxes were dealt with. Jason held the empty box and gestured for Liam and Cameron to follow as he led the way to a back hallway and eventually exited the building.

Jesse was already outside, a few of his men gathered around the two paper boxes. They'd set up lighting so they could more easily see what they were doing. Shifters had excellent night vision, but when it came to something this delicate, it was helpful to have bright lights and magnification. Jesse had both at the ready. They were working at a picnic table set some distance from the Pack house.

Nobody was talking. Everything was being done in silence. As Jason deposited the empty box onto the table next to the two full ones, Liam ran his detector over them with no result. Everyone looked at Cameron, and he made the glyph and held it on the boxes. Liam ran his detector over them again with very different results.

As he zeroed in on the locations of the three problem spots—one on each box in very different positions, but well camouflaged by the bold printing and magic—Cameron moved closer to get a good look. There, in the tiniest size possible with the human hand were magical glyphs of obscurement, formed in a small circle, hand-written in black ink on the thick black lines of the printed pattern. The devices were hidden within.

Cameron had to break that circle of obscurement first. Only then, would the mundane electronic device be visible without his input of magic. He pointed to himself and reached into his pocket. He had an obsidian stone that would work perfectly for this. Charged in the Light of the Goddess, it would absorb the small magic of the circle of glyphs into itself as soon as he scratched a line through one of the characters. To that end, he also took out his pocketknife and set to work.

Placing the stone on the box in just the right position, he scratched through the small glyph circle and felt the release of the magic into the stone. He repeated the action twice more and then moved back. Liam stepped up and, with his own pocketknife, cut out a small electronic device from each of the three boxes. They had been embedded into the cardboard and painted over in black, though once the obscuring magic was negated, they were easily visible to the naked eye.

Bugs, Cameron thought they were called. Electronic listening devices. The wolves had been wise to do this all in silence.

One of Jesse's men held up a glass jar filled with some liquid and handed it to Liam. Liam looked to Jason, and the Alpha stepped closer as Liam opened the lid of the jar. Cameron smelled something noxious, and the wolves winced a little, their noses much more sensitive than Cameron's. Jason looked at all three of the little devices, which had been laid out on the picnic table. Nobody had touched them with anything other than tweezers and blades. Jason looked both enraged and determined.

"You've trespassed into the heart of my Pack," Jason said aloud, clearly seething with anger. "You have earned your death, and we will deliver it." Jason nodded at Jesse, who had a look of quiet fury on his face.

"The Wraiths are coming for you," was all he said, but the cold fire in his voice made Cameron want to shiver.

Then Jason nodded at Liam, and the blond man lifted the three bugs with tweezers and placed them one-by-one into the liquid in the jar. Little sparks and fizzes told Cameron that whatever power source they'd had was destroyed by the liquid, whatever it was.

"They're dead," Liam reported, sealing the jar. "I might be able to get a serial number off them and back-trace where they came from, but that's not really my specialty."

"That's okay, Liam. My mate is a detective, and if she can't track it down, she'll know somebody who can," Jason said, clapping Liam on the shoulder. "Thank you for this. I can't believe those things have been sitting there under my nose for weeks."

Jason came to stand before Cameron and held out his hand. "Thank you, Sir Cameron," the Alpha said formally, using Cameron's title. "We wouldn't have found those without your help."

Cameron shook the Alpha's hand, accepting his thanks. "If you have any more of that paper stored anywhere, Liam and I should probably check it over."

"I'll track that down tomorrow. I know we got a large office supply order a couple of months ago, but I'm not sure what it all was or where it all went. One of the maternals runs the office, and she'll be here in a few hours. We can check with her then, after we've all had a chance to get an hour or two of rest." The Alpha turned to the men and thanked them all, telling them to be on alert and sending them on their way.

Liam went with the rest of the Wraiths back up the mountain to the Wraiths' part of Pack territory. Jesse remained with his brother and Cameron, and the three of them headed back to the Pack house. They left the boxes on the table for now. It was a clear night with no rain, so the wrapped reams of paper in the full boxes would come to no harm from a few hours outside.

When Cameron returned to the suite, he found Kaleen sitting in front of the television in the main room, watching the weather report. She looked at him and smiled when he shut the door behind himself.

"I'm surprised to find you up," Cameron said, just to make conversation.

She looked good enough to eat. She'd obviously had a shower and a change of clothes. She looked warm and cuddly, snuggled into one corner of the sofa. He really wanted to join her there, but he didn't want to push things too hard or too far.

"I don't sleep a lot, in general," she replied, shrugging. "I was wondering..." She looked away, as if in trepidation.

"What?" He moved closer, gentling his tone to coax whatever it was she was hesitant to say out of her.

"I'd really like to take a walk outside. In the woods. Do you think that would be okay?" She looked back, meeting his gaze. "All those hours in the car. I feel the need to stretch my legs and connect with the trees."

Cameron frowned a bit, considering. "It's not a hundred percent safe out there. The enemy has attacked here recently."

"I know, which is why I waited to see what you thought of the idea," she told him.

Oh, he liked that. He liked that very much. She had waited for him.

"I suppose..." He thought about it and decided, why not? "If you wouldn't mind having me along for company, we could take a stroll through the woods. I'm sure the Pack has extra patrols out there in both human and wolf form, but I'd like to make sure no harm comes to you."

She smiled at his words and leapt up from the sofa. "Great. Can we go now, or do you need to do anything here first?"

"No time like the present," Cameron replied, grinning a bit at her eagerness. He opened the door to the suite and bowed slightly as she approached and then went through the door and out into the hallway.

Chapter Eleven

K aleen breathed in the fresh mountain air and rejoiced. Her heart needed this. A few minutes in nature, and she would rest easier. It had been a long journey filled with uncertainty. Now, she was in this new, welcoming place, and she needed a few minutes to get to know the rhythm of this forest, the sound of its song. Only then, would she feel completely comfortable here.

She needed to know the forest, and the forest needed to know her. It was vital that they come to an understanding, at least on her part.

Under the influence of the forest night, Kaleen felt herself relaxing for the first time in days. As she grew more comfortable, she allowed herself to remember the dreamy kiss she had shared with Cameron. He hadn't mentioned it, and neither had she, but oh, man, she'd been thinking about it. A lot.

The kiss in the garden hadn't been nearly as hot or steamy, though it had been sweet in its own way. Still, the half-awake kiss had been... Tempestuous. She wanted to kiss him again and see if it was as perfect as she remembered. She knew that way lay danger. He was full-blooded fey and, as such, not for her, but that didn't mean she couldn't...experiment...a little, just while he was here. Right?

"'Tis a beautiful territory this wolf Pack has staked out," Cameron said quietly as they walked along. The lilt of his slight brogue was more prevalent when he relaxed, she noticed.

She liked knowing these little things about him. It made their relationship seem more intimate, somehow, though they'd only really just met a short time ago. Still, she felt like she already knew some very fundamental truths about Cameron. He was a good man, despite being full-fey.

"I like this forest," she replied, looking around at the dark trees, emitting a kind of light energy that wreathed the world in shades of greens and golds to her special night vision.

She didn't know how Cameron saw it, but she knew fey had excellent night vision too. Neither of them had the limitations of humanity when it came to the nighttime hours. They slept little, and the night was not a stranger, just another flavor of the mortal realm that was usually quieter and somehow more mysterious than daytime.

"We are nearing where Leonora rests, awaiting rescue and rejuvenation," Cameron said softly.

"She rests in a willow, you said," Kaleen confirmed, remembering all that she'd been told about her many-times-over great-grandmother.

"Aye, she does, but I was able to communicate with her for just a moment before I left to find you. She is holding up, but you ladies will need to perform the rite as soon as possible to give her the best chance at a full recovery," he admitted.

Kaleen heard the sense of urgency in his voice and realized the situation was a bit worse than she'd thought. Perhaps he'd been downplaying the severity of the situation with the others in order not to worry them before all the women were assembled and ready to do the spell. It felt good that he was sharing the truth of the matter with her. She was, after all, the final chess piece—the final dryad descendant they'd needed to find and convince to assist. Now that she was here, they could gather everybody together and get on with things.

They walked on in silence, but the forest was anything but silent to Kaleen's senses. She could hear the song of the trees and the whispers of the earth as they walked along. She felt her tension melting away until it was completely gone, and only then, could she open herself completely to the wonder of this forest.

This forest that had known the presence of a full-blooded dryad for a very long time. This was Leonora's forest. It protected her as she had protected it, and it was much more...sentient...for lack of a better word, than any other woodland Kaleen had ever experienced.

And it welcomed Kaleen in a joyful way that made her smile in wonder. It recognized her blood. Her heritage. Her ancestry. It knew she was a descendant of its dear friend, Leonora. It knew Kaleen was here to help, and it welcomed her wholeheartedly.

For a moment, she stood still, nearly overwhelmed by the flood over her senses. The sighs of the leaves, the scent of pine in the air, the squish of loamy earth under her feet. Everything worked together to speak the truth of this patch of woodland. This blessed place where a dryad had lived for centuries and imbued the earth with her own magic and healing touch.

Tears rolled down Kaleen's cheeks as she stood under the wash of all the sensory input and felt the wildwood's sorrow and concern over the fate of its beloved friend, Leonora. It mourned and felt...not exactly fear, but something like trepidation...for Leonora's current predicament. It wanted her back, and it wanted her back to full strength. It wanted her joyful and happy once again, and it communicated that desire to Kaleen in no uncertain terms.

"What is it? Are you all right, lass?" Cameron's voice came to her out of the mist that had descended over her senses. His voice pulled her back.

Cameron was standing in front of her, his hands on her upper arms, unease on his handsome face, that red hair of his gleaming, even in the dark of night. His grip was strong, but not harmful. His brows were drawn together in concern.

"I'm okay," she replied slowly, coming back to herself little by little. She hadn't realized she'd been so far gone in the song of the forest. "Sorry. It's just..." She shook her head slightly, trying to dial back the sound from the forest and its impact on her senses. "I was a little overwhelmed for a moment. The woodland really misses Leonora and wants her back. It wanted me to know how much."

Cameron's expression lightened. "Came on a bit too strong, eh?" He tilted his head to the side and looked up at the trees. "Give her a break, lads. This little sparrow is much more sensitive to the likes of you than the other lasses you've met recently."

Oddly enough, his words seemed to have some effect as the forest drew back some of its urgent whispers. It tamped itself down a bit to a much more manageable level, and she felt more herself within moments. She looked up at Cameron, stepping closer and placing her hands on his chest.

"I didn't know you could do that," she said, wonder in her voice. "Thank you."

He didn't back away, and his hands went from gripping her upper arms to sliding up to her shoulders, caressing gently. He had such strong hands. She wondered what they would feel like on her most tender parts.

Which made her think of that kiss they'd shared when she'd been half asleep. Again. Had her foggy memories of that kiss built it up in her mind to something it hadn't really been? There really was only one way to find out.

She had to kiss him again. And standing so close to him in the romantic ethereal light of the forest night, she felt like she really *had* to kiss him again, though she knew she probably shouldn't.

"I'm no dryad, but I do know a thing or two about magic," he replied with a little grin that made her want to kiss the curve of his lips, to see if he tasted as good as she remembered.

Why not? This was a once-in-a-lifetime moment. A once-in-a-lifetime man. She might as well seize the opportunity that would probably never come again. She leaned into him and raised up on her tiptoes, matching her lips to his.

Kaleen could tell she'd surprised him by the briefest moment of hesitation before he joined fully in the kiss. Then, it was everything she'd thought she'd remembered from that half-asleep dream kiss...and more.

The sensations she remembered were even more intense and enthralling. He tasted of magic and mystery, temptation and desire. His arms came around her, his embrace making her feel small and delicate and...cherished. No man had ever made her feel so special, so precious. No man she had known before had ever seemed to care enough about what she was feeling to make sure she enjoyed intimacy of even the simplest nature as much as he did.

Cameron was special in that regard. He seemed to put her feelings and comfort first, touching her gently and enticing her response in subtle, delicious ways. He stroked his fingers over her shoulders and then down her back, sending pleasurable shivers down her spine. Then, his hands settled at her waist, the warm strength of his touch a gentle pressure that let her know he was there and ready for whatever might come next.

Meanwhile, his lips traced hers, his tongue seeking entrance to her mouth, which it was granted in due course. When they were open to one another, there was no holding back. The kiss turned tempestuous in an instant, his hands lowering to cup her butt, pulling her against him so she could feel his hardness against her softness. It was thrilling. It was empowering.

For the first time in her life, Kaleen felt a little bit like some kind of femme fatale, able to make even the strongest man swoon with desire. Not that Cameron was swooning. Far from it. His masculine power was enough to make *her* want to swoon, and she'd never done such a foolish thing in her entire life!

"Sorry to interrupt." A male voice came to Kaleen's ears out of the dark night. She jumped and moved away from Cameron, feeling somehow guilty to have been caught necking like a teenager.

Cameron moved slightly in front of her, blocking the newcomer's view of her while she got herself together. She wasn't too disheveled physically, but mentally, she was all over the place.

"Master Dmitri," Cameron acknowledged the other man in a friendly but slightly guarded way. "It's been a while."

The newcomer walked a bit closer where Kaleen could get a better look at him. He was tall, dark and handsome. Par for the course among the wolf Pack. Almost every last one of the shifters had movie-star good looks and physiques to match.

"Sir Cameron," the man named Dmitri nodded politely. "It is good to see you again. I see you have one of my friend's descendants with you whom I have not yet met." Dmitri nodded toward Kaleen with a curious expression on his handsome face.

"You're friends with Leonora?" Kaleen asked, stepping out to stand next to Cameron, feeling as if she needed to assert herself with this other man for some reason. She didn't want to give anybody here the impression that she was a pushover or anything like that.

"Indeed. I was here when she was wounded and asked to be put into the willow to save her life. I gave her a few drops of my blood to help preserve her existence and promised to keep watch by night so that no harm came to her resting place," he informed her.

Kaleen was impressed, and a bit confused. If he gave her his blood, he must be some sort of magical being she hadn't yet encountered. The only thing she could think of from her mother's teachings was...

"You're a bloodletter?"

She blurted it out. Not at all politely. Kaleen shook her head at her own lack of proper etiquette. Her mother had warned her that vampires were sticklers for manners, and here, she'd acted the fool the first time she'd met one. Her mother would not be happy with Kaleen's behavior.

But Dmitri seemed not to take offense. He merely smiled a little and tilted his head.

"I'm sorry. I'm Kaleen Fairchild, and I'm usually not quite so rude. My mother told me about your kind, but I have never met a bloodletter before. I know my ignorance is no excuse, but I confess, I'm a bit...uh...frazzled at the moment," she admitted, her face heating with a blush the bloodletter could no doubt sense in some way, even in the dark. He had to have as good night vision as she and Cameron did, but she didn't dare ask him anything after her initial blunder.

"Fairchild, you say?" Dmitri looked to Cameron and back to Kaleen. "You are part-fey?"

Now, that was rude too, but she figured she owed him that much, at least, after her own disgraceful conduct. Not that two wrongs made a right, but all the formality of the magical world had always struck Kaleen as a bit silly. Even as her mother had impressed upon her the need to be respectful of Others at all times, Kaleen had wondered why everybody had to walk on eggshells around each other. They all had magic of one kind or another, shouldn't that be more uniting than dividing? Shouldn't they all just be able to be friends and get along without all the formality? Her mother had never really had a good answer for that one.

"My mother is fey," Kaleen admitted. "And I surmise from the way Cameron addressed you, that you are the Master of this region, since you seem well acquainted with the area. You must also be allied with the wolf Pack to be so free with their territory." Her brain was working again, and she was trying to make up for her earlier blunder. "I'm pleased to make your acquaintance."

Dmitri bowed slightly. "As am I, milady. I am glad you have come to join your magic to the others and attempt to free my friend, Leonora. She has waited a long time for rescue."

"We'll do our best," she replied, feeling determination fill her. They had to succeed. They just *had* to.

"If they all get here in time, we plan to do the rite at moonrise tomorrow. I believe that's just before midnight. If not tomorrow, then the following night," Cameron told the other man.

"I will be here to watch over your work, then," Dmitri said with decision in his tone.

"I was hoping you would say that," Cameron admitted. "We could use some air cover since we know the enemy knows of this place. It would make sense that they'd try something if they have any inkling of what we plan to do. We've found electronic listening devices hidden by magical means on some of the office supplies, so we can't be certain how much the *Venifucus* know of our plans."

Dmitri frowned. "Mundane electronics hidden by magical means? No wonder the enemy knows so much. I confess, I am relieved to hear that it's not some member of the Pack turned rogue. That would have been heartbreaking for the wolves, and unsettling to the Pack structure."

"No doubt about that," Cameron agreed. "But it still leaves us with the problem that those listening devices have been in the Pack house and the business office for some time. It's hard to know how much the enemy has already learned and how it will be used against us."

"I will assist in whatever way I can. I promised that to Leonora when she went into the tree, and I count her among my oldest and dearest friends. I can do no other than live up to my word," Dmitri told them.

"Thank you, my friend," Cameron told the Master vampire.

It was strange to think that a fey was actually friends with a bloodletter. According to what her mother had told her about them, Kaleen wouldn't have expected that. Not at all.

Her mother had taught her that the magical races didn't have much to do with each other at all, if they could help it. Of course, things were changing now that the enemy was out in the open, challenging the status quo at every turn, trying to bring the worst kind of evil back to the world of man.

"It was good to meet you, milady. Rest easy knowing that I will guard your ancestor's resting place tonight, along with the wolves. Nothing will get past us this night, and perhaps by this time tomorrow, Leonora will finally be free," Dmitri said, offering a hopeful twist of his lips.

"I pray you're right, Master Dmitri. Thanks for looking after her," Kaleen replied.

"My pleasure," he answered, dipping his head in that old-world way he had about him.

"It was nice meeting you," she added as he turned to go. He looked back once, then faded into the forest as if he'd never even been there.

Chapter Twelve

K aleen saw it, but she didn't quite believe it. She figured that vampires had a different kind of magic than she'd ever seen before, but it was still startling to see the way he used it. She'd never seen anyone fade from view quite that way. It was...unnatural. Somewhat unnerving too. She shivered.

Cameron chuckled low. "Don't let him get to you, lass. I think he was just showing off a bit to impress you."

"It worked," Kaleen replied honestly, still looking where the vampire had faded away.

"Shall we go back to the house?" Cameron asked in a quiet tone that immediately made her think of their interrupted kiss.

Just like that, she forgot about the show-off vampire, and her blood heated with renewed desire. She definitely wanted to go back to the house and pick up where they'd left off—if he'd play along.

She wasn't entirely sure if that's what he'd meant to imply. Maybe he was just suggesting going inside and going to bed. Separately.

What a disappointment that would be. After learning the truth about his kiss—that it was even better than she remembered from those first encounters—she wanted to experience more of his passion. More of his desire. More of his lovemaking.

"Yes," she answered slowly. "Let's."

She held out her hand, and he took it. Was he agreeing to what she hoped he was agreeing to? She'd find out soon enough, when they got back to their suite.

They arrived back at the Pack house quickly. Had she been hurrying? She wasn't sure. She knew her eagerness was palpable. She wondered if he felt it too.

As they went up the stairs to the guest suite, she wasn't sure what to expect. She would be crushed if he simply said good night and went to his own bed. Alone. Yet, she didn't really know how to pick up where they'd left off in the forest before Master Dmitri had arrived. The moment had been lost. She was afraid it had been lost forever.

She felt shy and awkward as he opened the door to the suite. She didn't know what to do to recoup the feelings they'd shared just a few minutes before. She wasn't even sure if they were on the same wavelength anymore.

The moment the door closed behind them, Cameron swept her into his arms, and all her worries dissipated. As usual, she been overthinking things. His lips claimed hers, and then, all thoughts fled from her mind. There was only feeling. The intense desire that only Cameron had ever elicited in her. She wanted more. She wanted to see this to its logical conclusion and find out if she was right about him.

She sensed he could finally show her all the things she'd been missing. He'd already aroused her more than any other man she had known, and they'd barely even gotten started. There was something so compelling about him. So...familiar, in a way. She couldn't quite explain it, even to herself.

She responded to him, allowing him to take the kiss deeper. She clung to him, enjoying the feeling of his warm, hard body next to hers. But there was too much fabric in the way.

Even as he pushed her up against the wall next to the door, she reached for his shirt, wanting it gone. He kissed her deep and wild. He rubbed against her body, even as she tried to rid him of his clothing. They were both desperate for each other, and his urgency definitely echoed hers.

"Do you want this, little sparrow?" he asked, coming up for air and breathing hard. "Do you want me?" His tone was gentle. Hopeful. She felt it down to her bones.

"I do," she said, realizing only in that moment how much like a vow her words sounded. "I want to be with you, Cameron."

A fire kindled in his eyes, and she felt the answering conflagration down deep in her soul. He stepped back, and for a fleeting moment, she thought he was going to leave her. Thankfully, she was wrong. He swept her into his arms, carrying her as if she weighed nothing at all, and walked swiftly to the bedroom he'd been using.

He placed her on her feet at the side of the bed and then spent delectable moments relieving them both of their clothing. He would pause now and again to kiss the skin he had uncovered or join his mouth to hers in a lingering salute. The urgency had been tamped down, but it was still there. Within moments, they were both naked, and she stepped close to him, rubbing her body against his, loving the friction between them.

She was soft where he was hard. So very hard. She looked down, admiring the view. He was well formed and larger than the few boys she'd dated in high school. She got the idea that this experience was going to be completely different than anything that had come before. She couldn't wait.

She bent her knee and put one leg behind her on the bed, sliding backwards and tugging him gently with one hand, so that he would follow her. They knelt at the center of the large bed and kissed, hands entwined as their lips rediscovered everything they had already learned about each other.

Now that the moment was upon them, Cameron seemed to want to take things slowly. That would never do. Kaleen didn't want to wait any longer. She wanted to know everything, all at once. She wanted to discover the secrets of passion that had been hidden from her for so long.

She freed one hand and reached downward between them, grasping his hardness in her fingers. He felt warm against her palm. Hard and pulsing with life. She wanted to feel him even more intimately. She squeezed slightly, and he groaned, even as he kissed her, his careful control seeming to slip into something much more wanton.

Good. That's more like it.

She leaned backward, urging him to follow her down onto the bed. He complied, breaking the kiss only to run his mouth over her breasts, then farther down her body. She had to let go of his cock as he moved away, but she had little time to regret it as he spread her legs and placed his mouth on her.

Kaleen nearly came off the bed as her back arched so high at the immediate pleasure he brought her. She'd never felt that kind of reaction before. Of course, none of her few encounters had included anything quite so...creative...before. The few men—boys, really—that she'd been with had been rather pedestrian in their tastes. Perhaps it was because they hadn't had much experience. Just like her. She'd been awfully young, and so had they.

Cameron, though, he was experienced. Much older than her. With the warrior's lifestyle and, no doubt, a warrior's tastes in bed sport. Her body tingled as she thought of it. She imagined there were a lot of things he could show her. Like what he was doing right now. Sweet Mother of All! That felt *so* good.

Then, he thrust his finger into her as his tongue teased her. She whimpered as pleasure almost overcame her.

"Cameron! Please!" was all she could manage, but he seemed to understand.

He raised up, grinning at her, his finger still sliding in and out of her as their eyes met and held. He was between her splayed thighs as if he belonged there.

Perhaps he did. Now, there was an odd thought.

"Do you want to fuck?" he asked, his crude word sending more tingles down her spine. His face looked raw, his expression as fierce as she'd ever seen it, though his eyes held a teasing glint that reassured her.

"Yes!" she gasped as his finger found a particular spot inside her that made her squirm in heightened desire.

"Say it, lass. I need to hear it," he fairly growled.

"I... I want you to fuck me, Cameron. Fuck me hard." She said it, and the words sent a little thrill through her that she never would have expected. Who knew such things could heighten pleasure? She never would've believed it, if she hadn't been experiencing it at that very moment.

"Never say I let a lady down," he muttered, winking once at her in a reassuring way as he moved closer, removing his finger and positioning his thick shaft at the apex of her thighs.

He said nothing more as he inched his way inside, pushing steadily in a way that made everything all right. So very all right. When he was seated fully, he held her gaze a moment longer.

"You okay?" he asked, his breathing coming short.

"Fine," she replied, panting a little. "Better than ever, in fact." Was that her voice—all breathy and flirtatious?

Cameron smiled in a devilish way. "Good. Now, let's work on making that *fine* into something more like *outstanding*."

She giggled a little, and then, he started moving. Slow, at first. Then increasing in speed and strength as they went along. She almost forgot how to breathe at one point, but instinct kicked in, and she matched him move for move. She surprised herself with how natural it felt. Sex had never been like this before. Not for her. Which was why she'd never felt all that interested in it.

She hadn't missed it. All those years living alone. But now, she began to understand that the right partner made all the difference in the world.

He pressed into her, driving her passion higher with each powerful thrust until she didn't know where he left off and she began. She felt like she was part of him and he of her. Like their union was forged in the earth, for all time.

Silly, really. She knew that was just some kind of fantasy, but at the moment, it felt *right*. He felt right. Like she never wanted to be parted from him.

Which was impossible. But all thoughts fled as he put one big hand between them and started stroking that little button that sent her right over the edge into oblivion. A moment later, she felt him tense as he joined her there in that space between the stars where pleasure and passion sent the luckiest of lovers.

A place she had never really been before. Not like this.

Cameron lay in the bed, Kaleen asleep beside him. Everything had changed in such a short time. He held up his arm and realized the mating mark he had worn for a thousand years was completely gone. Just as his sorrow over losing

Molly was gone. Healed by the new woman in his life. The woman in bed next to him.

She hadn't replaced Molly, per se. She'd just come into his life and reminded him how to live again. How to love and be part of this world he had chosen. How to give of his heart and not just his strength. She had taught him so much without even trying.

This, he realized, was what love was meant to be. An equal sharing. A reciprocal relationship where each gave to the other without effort. He wanted to bask in the joy flooding his heart but there was still so much to go through. They faced untold danger and it was possible one or both of them might not live through it.

With one last look at his arm, he sighed deeply. Molly was well and truly gone. Only Kaleen remained and he would keep her with him as long as possible. Forever...if they were given the chance. But for now, all they had was this moment before the storm. This time out of time where nothing mattered but the two of them.

He rolled over and tugged her into his arms, falling asleep as she slept on. Together. At least, for now.

The next morning, Kaleen was pleased to find that all of the dryad cousins had arrived by the time she and Cameron went down for a late breakfast. More of a brunch, really. They'd lazed around in the early morning hours, making love and just enjoying each other. She'd never really had the leisure to do that before with either of the two men who'd briefly shared her bed in the past.

Now that she knew what she was missing, she'd never settle for the wham-bam-forget-you-ma'am style of relationship she'd had in the past. It could be that being with Cameron had ruined her for any other man, but if that really was the case, she wouldn't worry about it now. No, right now, she was going to just enjoy being with him for as long as it lasted. No sense worrying about a future that might never come to pass.

Heck, they might fail miserably today and be flattened by a backlash of their own magic. Bad things did happen, and she'd be a fool to think the future was guaranteed. Her own family situation was proof that it wasn't, for sure.

Kaleen was introduced to Cece and her mate, Deke, who were also grabbing a meal in the Pack house's dining hall since they'd only just arrived. Deke had flown them in from California, and they were both hungry from travel and just sitting down to eat when Kaleen and Cameron arrived in the dining room. Sally was already sitting at their table and waved Kaleen and Cameron over, making the introductions.

Before too much longer, Kaleen and Cameron had collected their plates from the breakfast buffet, which was still out, though a bit smaller than it had been earlier in the day. They rejoined the table and sat with Cece and Deke, spending a few minutes getting to know one another.

Kaleen liked Cece right off, and her husband seemed like a really nice man, though he was a bit quiet at first. He let his mate do the talking, and Kaleen wasn't surprised to learn that Deke was fully human, though he'd been raised in a family of water elementals. Cameron had told Kaleen a bit of the story earlier, and it was good to have a face to go with the details.

While they were still at the table, two more dryad descendants arrived. Sunny was Sally's long-lost sister, and Crystal was another cousin. Both were incredibly nice, and both had mates that were off somewhere, doing something else. Crystal claimed that her mate, Marco, was checking out the wine cellar and adding the cases of wine he'd brought with them to the stock. Sunny's mate, Den, was checking in with the Wraiths, farther up the mountain, since they were old friends and military comrades.

"When did you get in?" Cece asked Sunny. "We would have offered you a ride, but Deke said Den told him you guys weren't even in California."

"We were visiting Crystal and Marco in Nebraska," Sunny clarified. "I really didn't think this would all come together so fast, or I'd have changed our travel plans a bit. Still, it all worked out. We flew in with Crystal and Marco late last night."

They all chatted for a while, getting to know each other a little. Kaleen was impressed by all her newfound cousins. They all seemed like very nice people, each with a different background and life experience that made them very interesting and knowledgeable about a wide range of topics. Sunny was a former

ballerina and had the willow grace to prove it. Cece lived on a mountain in
California, and Crystal had been in hotel management before meeting Marco.

About the time they were finished eating and lingering over a second cup of
coffee, Pam and Maria came into the dining room. They both lived a bit farther
up the mountain with their Wraith mates and had likely driven down together.

Once Deke heard that Arlo and Jesse were in the office with the other men, he
excused himself and headed out of the dining room. That left all the part-dryad
women around a big table...with Cameron.

Chapter Thirteen

"Now that we've got you all here," Cameron said, looking around at the gathered might of the seven part-dryads, "perhaps we can go over everyone's role in the spell casting and see if we can get some of the tools that might be useful in the work."

"That sounds like a great idea," Sally said enthusiastically. "High Priestess Bettina told me a little bit about it, but I'm really glad you're here to walk us through. It sounded way too complicated to try on our own without guidance, and though Bettina said she'd do her best to come here when the time came, from what I understand, there's something going on where she is right now that would make it hard for her to leave."

"I talked with Bettina about this before I went to help Pam and Arlo in Idaho," Cameron admitted. "She turned over the task to me, and I accepted her commission. I am well-versed in the spell and can help you all perform it. But there are a few things we will need to prepare."

What followed was a strategy session mixed with what felt like a pre-game briefing. Cameron enjoyed how well the part-dryads listened, and they even asked very astute questions. He used a paper napkin to sketch out the approximate positions they would each take when they cast the spell.

"The Elven Star is a seven-pointed star," he told them, drawing it on the napkin. "Each of you will take one point, with Leonora's willow tree at the center.

Ideally, each of you will have a representative stone. We should look around and see if anyone has some that we can borrow for this purpose. We'll need representative colors. Red can be ruby, jasper or carnelian, yellow citrine or tiger eye, green can be emerald or jade, light blue could be turquoise or aquamarine, though blue topaz could also work, dark blue lapis lazuli or sapphire. For purple, amethyst is probably the easiest to find. And finally, we'll need some clear quartz. White diamond would also work. The important part is the color of the stone. We can make substitutions if we must, but chances are, if we ask around the Pack, someone will have jewelry or some kind of keepsake made from these stones that we can borrow."

"Will the items come to any sort of harm? I'd hate to use something someone holds precious, only to return it to them damaged," Maria said.

"If we do this right, the stones will help channel the power. They'll go back to their owners purified and charged with high magic. I believe they will become objects of protection after their use in such a strong spell," Cameron told them. "The only way they could become damaged is if we fail."

Everybody was silent a moment. Sally put her hand down on the table. "Then we don't fail."

The others nodded, agreeing silently with her.

It was a bit of a scavenger hunt at that point, as people searched their own jewelry boxes and curio cabinets first to come up with the needed stones. Sally had a necklace of carnelian beads, as well as a large, very clear quartz crystal point and a piece of an amethyst geode to contribute. Maria, likewise, had a necklace of deep green jade beads in her jewelry box, as well as an amethyst pendant. Crystal was wearing an aquamarine ring given to her by her new mate as a gift. It was an heirloom from his family, very old and magical in its own right.

Sunny had large citrine ring set in an old-fashioned gold setting that would suffice. Cece was wearing a pendant with a large lapis cabochon at its center.

"I decided to take this with me when we left, but I didn't know why," Cece admitted. "My father said it was a family heirloom," she added, patting the large gold pendant with the handsome stone.

Once they had all the stones, Cameron set them searching for other things they would need. A small brazier or something like it that could contain a little fire. A shallow copper dish that they could fill with water. A dagger that could be used as an athame—a magical and symbolic blade used to cut magical ties. Enough salt to cast a wide circle of protection around them all, and a few different herbs and other substances that were easily found in the forest.

As the items were gathered, Cameron drew out a small sketch of where everything and everyone should be positioned when the time came to do the spell. They used the big round table in one corner of the dining room as their workspace, and the work group came in and out as they found the items that were needed.

Finally, everything was assembled, and Cameron talked them through the plan. He even had them rehearse where they would stand, using one of the smaller tables as a stand-in for the willow tree around which they would stand that night. He couldn't invoke the actual spell. That would be pointless, but he could at least help the ladies get used to where they would be standing and what it might feel like.

The pressure was on to get this right the first time. They might possibly have a chance at a do-over, but nothing was guaranteed. The likelihood of the enemy interfering in any second attempt was high, considering any first attempt would stir up a whole lot of magic that would *not* go unnoticed. Also, Leonora really needed the infusion of magic to save her life. She was fading and might not have time for them to mess up. They had to get this right.

When they'd rehearsed everything they could and had their positions and roles in this endeavor figured out as best they could without actually doing the spell, it was just about dinner time. Cameron realized they'd been at this most of the day, and everybody was looking a little weary and stressed. Not good.

"Okay," he said, getting everyone's attention as they came back to the table. "You've done good work today, but now, we need to gear up for tonight. I see they're laying out the buffet, and it's good for us to eat early and well, then perhaps have a bit of a lie down for a while. Best time for this spell is at moonrise, which is right around midnight tonight. Let's eat together and settle any outstanding questions, then I think you should all go rest for a bit. We can reconvene here at about eleven-fifteen tonight, and we'll all go down to the willow together. Sound good?"

Nods all around answered him, and the dining room started filling up with others who were staying at the Pack house for whatever reason. The part-dryads' mates started showing up, taking their places next to their ladies. Everybody got food at the buffet, except for Marco, though he came back with a bottle of very fine wine from the kitchen and a few glasses.

The dinner was subdued for the most part. The ladies had put in a full day and were asking the occasional question about details they wanted to nail down before tonight. Every one of them had a little bag of things they would be responsible for bringing to the site. The stones, herbs and other equipment they'd gathered during the day. All seven of the ladies knew what to do with their particular assortment of goodies now, and they would make sure all was in readiness—each responsible for their own part of the preparation.

They had a nice dinner, then everybody dispersed to their rooms. Each had been given a place to rest in the Pack house so that everyone could stay in one place before the big event.

Cameron and Kaleen went back to their suite after dinner. She'd been by his side most of the day, which had felt really great. He never grew impatient or annoyed. Quite the contrary, in fact. Her presence comforted him on some basic level that he hadn't even been aware of before now.

She was good to have around. Comforting. And challenging to his intellect in a stimulating way that he really enjoyed. She was also beautiful inside and out. He liked everything about her, which wasn't something he'd said often about anyone in any realm. Kaleen was something really special and entirely unique in his experience. A woman who just...fit...into his life and at his side.

He could easily envision her there, at his side. Forever.

A big thought for such a short acquaintance. He was not shifter to know his mate on first sight or sniff or whatever it was the shifters did. Among the fey marriages were often made for political reasons among members of the High

Court. At least in Cameron's family. Kaleen's as well, though she didn't seem to know it.

She'd been raised human in the mortal realm. What did she really know of the fey, except what her mother had told her? Kaleen probably had no idea of the standing of their respective families and the suitability of their political positions wasn't something that was even on her radar, as the humans said.

"I know you don't need much sleep," Cameron began speaking as soon as their suite's door closed behind them, "but you should try to rest a bit before tonight."

"I will if you will," Kaleen told him, holding out her hand to him and offering a slight smile.

He took her hand. He would never turn down even the smallest act of intimacy with her. Not while they both breathed. He had quickly become addicted to her, though he still wasn't sure what to make of it.

"We can start in the bedroom, but then, I think we should try out a ritual bath," he said, his eyes sparkling at her with deviltry.

"A ritual bath?" she repeated, enjoying his mood. "You're making that up."

He tilted his head to one side as if considering. "Yes and no. It's always good to go into a major spell casting as clean as possible. Ritually washing away the past and starting the future fresh, so to speak, is a good thing, and I think we should do it, but I also think it'll be a lot more fun doing so together. That shower in there is large enough for two. I've been thinking about sharing it with you since we were put in this suite," he admitted.

"You have?" She hadn't realized he'd been thinking scandalous thoughts about that big shower stall...just as she had.

"I have," he said, grabbing her gently around the waist and swinging her around playfully. "Shall we try it out now or wait until later?"

"Now," she replied, enthusiastically. "You've got my mind spinning with all the possibilities."

"Then come with me, little sparrow," he teased, grinning as he crooked his finger and led her toward the spacious bathroom that lay between their two bedrooms in this well-appointed guest suite.

With a giggle, she followed him, only to have him round on her playfully, tugging her into his arms as he kissed her senseless the moment she was inside the room. He lifted her, his hands on her ass, squeezing before he placed her on the counter. He parted her thighs and stepped between, taking up the kiss once more. Only this time, he was undressing her as he went, ridding her of her shirt, then her bra.

Cameron paused at that point to admire and fondle her breasts, dipping his head to kiss her softness. She tugged at his shirt, hoping to see and touch more of his skin too. He took the hint and stepped back for a moment, pulling his shirt up and off over his head in a sinuous move that nearly stole her breath. He was the sexiest man alive. The way his muscles rippled and bunched as he moved made her mouth water. He was handsome as sin, and he had to know the effect he had on her. His grin said it all as he came back to her. He lifted her hands one by one, kissed them and then laid them on his chest.

"I like feeling your hands on me too, little sparrow," he informed her, his eyes smoldering with intensity and a touch of mischief.

"That's good," she told him. "Because I like touching you. You know how handsome you are."

He looked truly surprised by her words. He stuttered a moment before he finally was able to answer.

"I— I'm glad you think so. Honestly, the red hair has always made me feel a bit self-conscious. It's not a common color among the fey, as you may know." His bashfulness was charming and very real. She couldn't believe he didn't realize how incredibly sexy he was.

Just one more fascinating facet to Sir Cameron le Fey. She realized how much she enjoyed learning more about him. She wanted to know everything but dared not hope for such favor. Their relationship—if you could even call it that—had to be fleeting by the very nature of who they both were. She was half-human and chose to live in the mortal realm. He might choose to live here now, but he was fully fey and would likely go back someday, to the realm of his birth. Even if they had a long-term affair, that's all it really could ever be. An affair.

She didn't stop to examine why that thought disturbed her so much. She didn't want to think about tomorrow or the next day or the next week or the next year. She wanted to focus only on this moment, right now. Really, that's all she had with her fey lover. The present.

And she did count it as a gift. *He* was a gift. A lover she never could have imagined in her ignorance. Any lover she'd taken before paled into insignificance after the passion he'd shown her.

"I love your red hair," she said, reaching up to run her fingers through it. "It's as fiery as your spirit."

"I'm glad you see it that way," he said, moving closer. "I think you are beautiful," he placed a small kiss on her lips, "my little sparrow." He zeroed in on her lips and kissed her again, this time with all the fiery passion she had just described.

She strained toward him, rubbing her breasts against his hard-muscled chest. Everything about him aroused her. She ran her hands over his chest, arms and back, but she wanted more. Her fingers went to the button of his trousers and wrestled with the stubborn fabric. After a few moments, he seemed to understand what she was after, and he broke the kiss and stepped away to remove his pants and boxers, his rampant cock springing free as he uncovered it.

Kaleen licked her lips. She wanted to taste him, but so far, he hadn't given her time to do that sort of inventory of his body. Truthfully, she wasn't sure she could wait any longer to have him inside her just now, but definitely later. Later, she would take him in her hand and then taste him and learn every inch of him intimately.

Even as she watched him, she shed her own pants and panties, wanting no more fabric between them. He came back to her, stepping between her thighs, and she realized they were at a perfect height. Cameron seemed to realize it right around the same time she did and grasped her hips, pulling her a little closer to the edge.

He brought one hand around to test her readiness, sliding into the slick wetness between her thighs. He smiled at her as he put one finger, then two into her. She whimpered, wanting more. She always wanted more, it seemed, when it came to this man. He was fast becoming an addiction.

"Are you ready?" he asked in a teasing tone. "You feel ready." Cameron removed his fingers from within her and brought them to his lips. A shiver went all the way down her spine. Damn. Every move he made just made her want him more.

"I'm ready," she told him, almost begging. "Don't make me wait." Yes, that was her breathy, impatient voice, urging him on.

He smiled and moved closer, guiding himself to the spot where she most wanted him. He watched the place where they joined, and she watched him. The intensity of his concentration lit her senses on fire. It was one thing to be taken. It was another to be watched as it was done.

When he was all the way in, he stopped and looked up to meet her gaze. "All right?" he asked, his breathing hitched with suppressed passion.

"Fine," she told him, gasping the word out as she willed him to move.

"There's that word again." He chuckled and shook his head just once. "I can see that I'm going to have to try harder."

Chapter Fourteen

Harder. Kaleen's mind got stuck on that word, and suddenly, that's all she wanted. For Cameron to press himself into her over and over. Harder and harder. Until they both blew apart and soared for the sky. Together.

Cameron seemed to understand. He began thrusting, slowly at first, allowing her time to acclimate, then harder and faster. His pace built steadily as her desire rose into a tower of flames within her body that only he could quench. He pressed onward as pleasure threatened to overtake her... And then, it did. She burst into flames of ecstasy, like the phoenix shooting upward toward the sun, only to burn in the fire of their shared climax and be reborn, hopefully to do it all again.

She clung tight to him as he held her just as close. She loved the way his strong arms felt around her and the amazing pleasure he had taught her to crave. When she could speak again and her breathing had slowed to a manageable level, she drew back and looked into his eyes.

"Are you ready for that ritual bathing now?" He was smiling in that way that made her want to give him everything.

She could only shake her head and chuckle as he lifted her and walked with her—still impaled on his semi-hard cock—into that giant shower stall. He reached behind her and deftly turned on the water, allowing it to hit him alone until it warmed up to a cozy temperature. She appreciated that.

With the water raining down around them, she began to feel the heat building again inside her, deep in her belly where they were still joined. She could feel him lengthening and thickening, readying for round two.

Cameron placed her back against the wall, and the contrast between his hot, hard body in front and the cold tile at her back almost made her yelp at first, until she got used to it. And Cameron provided more than enough distraction as he began moving within her almost immediately, rekindling the passion that had only recently been sated. Or so she'd thought.

It turned out that she was wanton for him. Perhaps only for him. She'd never recovered so quickly and craved more so fast. But Cameron had been teaching her all sorts of things about herself and her passions that she'd never known. He was the maestro, and he played her body like a fine violin. She was his willing instrument, and the music they made together was the most beautiful she had ever experienced.

Their lovemaking was longer this time, since the edge had been taken off by their encounter on the countertop. This time, they lingered, the warm water causing a seductive slickness between their skin that made the whole thing even more delicious and exciting.

Kaleen cried out his name when she came this time, and he followed soon after, riding her, pushing her back to the wall and holding her up with his hands on her ass, his fingers teasing the crevice between for a little added thrill.

She felt boneless as passion overcame them both, and she started to drift back to earth like the rain falling all around them from the big showerhead he'd turned on once the water was warm enough. It was a soothing sensation after the tumultuous ride to glory, and she reveled in the feelings and the man.

Kaleen was very much afraid that Cameron had truly ruined her for anyone else, but she found she didn't have the strength right then to worry about it over much. Tomorrow would take care of itself. In fact, given what they were going to attempt in just a few hours, this moment, right here and right now, might be all they got.

She tried not to think about that one way or the other. They had to succeed. They just had to. But worrying about it right this minute wouldn't help anything. She'd be better off relaxing with her lover who was, by every measure, truly extraordinary. She hugged him a little closer and let him take her wherever he wished.

That turned out to be a long, languid shower where he soaped up and ran his hands over every inch of her body. They made love again in a soapy shower of bubbles, sliding against each other in the most exciting way possible. She laughed at his antics, and he joined in, teasing her passions higher. She never knew the act of love could be fun as well as arousing. Another lesson for her from the master of her desire.

Kaleen and Cameron spent way too long in that spacious shower, but eventually, they got out and dried off to make love again in the giant bed. Then, and only then, did they doze off, catching a couple of hours of rest before their big performance scheduled for that night.

Kaleen felt about as ready as she ever would by the time they all met back together in the dining room just before it was time to go out. She was nervous. As were the rest of them. There was a tension in the air that permeated the entire Pack, not just the seven part-dryads and their mates. Everybody seemed to be on edge.

"Something's up," Cameron said in a low voice as he watched the wide archway and the hall beyond that bustled with more activity than usual.

Sally and Jason walked through the archway, and both of their expressions were a bit grim. They came right over to the table where the others had gathered, and Jason spoke.

"There have been a couple of suspected intrusions on the perimeter, though nothing concrete just yet." His frown deepened. "Jesse has all his troops mobilized along with the regular border guard from the Pack. So far, nobody has seen anything actionable, but it feels like somebody might be testing our perimeter in preparation for a strike."

Cameron shook his head. "The enemy has been one step ahead of you for a while now. You had to expect something like this. Nevertheless, we have to proceed."

"No question about that," Sally replied at once.

Some of the others looked worried, Kaleen noticed. But not Cameron. He looked suitably concerned, but also determined. They were going to do this thing, come hell or high water. She felt the same.

Kaleen saw that everybody had their little bag of goodies and was ready to go. Sally gave them a short pep talk, then led the way out the back door, taking the shortest route to Leonora's willow. Nobody talked as they walked along the forest path. Even the trees seemed to be holding their breaths in anticipation of...something.

There was magic in the air. It was one of those rare moments in time when all the world paused to see what would happen next. Kaleen felt it, and she was fairly certain everybody else did too.

They arrived at the willow tree and immediately took their positions around it. The willow was old. Its trunk was wide. Its branches many and draping to the ground in places. It was a beautiful tree that hid the heart of this forest, holding Leonora within itself, in the place between life and death.

Their mission was to retrieve her. Heal her, and the tree. Save her life, and the health of this forest and the many others Leonora had touched in her very long lifetime. Kaleen felt the import of what they were about to attempt. Nothing could stop them. Nothing *should* stop them, if at all possible. But she had a feeling the enemy would try.

They were all in position, each fiddling with their little bag of tricks, setting up their own workspace on their point of the Elven Star. Kaleen had been reading up on the formation. Humans had some magical knowledge—even if they didn't always realize its full potential. What she'd been able to find on the Internet had told her that the seven-pointed star was also called a Faery Star by some. It was also thought to be more powerful than the more common pentagram that was so popular with human followers of the old religions.

In the mortal realm, Christians had sometimes used this star to represent the time it took for the Creator to make the world. Some still used this complicated star to ward off and protect against evil. In modern religions, the number seven appeared with great frequency. From the seven heavens of Islam and Hinduism, the seven steps the Buddha took upon rising, the seven oceans, the seven continents, the seven colors of the rainbow, and so many other instances, the significance of the number seven could not be argued.

In this case, each of the part-dryads would take up a position roughly corresponding to the four cardinal points—north, south, east, and west—plus the additional spheres of above, below, and most importantly in this case, within. Each of these points had a representative color accompanied by the stone items they had been able to find, plus bundles of various herbs and plant parts.

Kaleen was setting up her own workspace when Cameron tapped her on the shoulder. She looked up at him, seeing the concern on his beloved face.

"I'm going to cast the circle," he told her. He already had a large sack of salt in his hands. "The minute I close the circle, begin. I don't think we have much time to waste."

"It'll be okay," she told him, feeling at that moment a sense of tranquility descending over her. She didn't know why she felt this way, but she somehow sensed that even though they may face difficulties, they would come through this all right. She hoped she wasn't just imagining it.

Reaching upward, she cupped his cheek and drew him down for a quick kiss. She wished she could've stayed like that forever, but there was too much to do, and too little time in which to do it. She let him go with a rueful smile.

"Be careful, and keep your eyes open," she cautioned him.

"You do the same, little sparrow." With a jaunty wink, he left her and set about his business.

She knew he would be casting a circle of protection around the entire tree and the star formation. Theoretically, nothing could enter the circle once he had sealed it. He would lay a line of salt as he spoke the ritual words walking around the perimeter. Only when he reached the point where he had started and joined the line of salt into a complete circle would the magical energy snap into place, protecting all within. At least, that was the theory. She had never seen one of these circles of protection in practice.

Cameron ran the line of salt and words of magic around the perimeter of the tree—and those ladies setting up around it, to do their magical work—as fast as he could. He had an impending sense of danger. They were not going to get away with doing the spell in peace. He could feel it in his bones. The enemy was coming. They were going to try and disrupt tonight's plans.

He would not let them.

Cameron decided in that moment that he would cast this circle of protection around the women but remain outside of it. He would supplement the forces already arrayed to protect those women, and their objective, even more. He could fight alongside the werewolves as long as he was outside the circle. And, if he'd done his job well enough this afternoon, those ladies didn't need him to tell them what to do. They had all the tools they needed, and he'd given them the knowledge and the words. They could manage the spell on their own, he was sure.

Each and every one of those women had impressed him with their strength of character, force of will, and intellectual abilities. They would get the job done. His job would be to make sure they had the chance. After all, he was a warrior, not necessarily a mage, though in the mortal realm his knowledge of fey magic was greater than almost anyone else's. His lineage made him magic, but his calling made him a warrior. If there was a fight to be had, he would be better off fighting it face-to-face.

All he had to do was finish closing the circle, and then, he could stand watch over the ladies—Kaleen, in particular. He would take up a position at her back, holding off anyone who would dare attack. At least, that was the plan.

Just before he could get to the place where he had started the circle, right behind Kaleen, a blast of energy came out of the trees, knocking Kaleen right off her feet. Cameron's heart nearly stopped, but she got up almost immediately, an annoyed scowl on her face as she brushed off her clothing and rubbed her sore bottom.

"That was uncalled for," she said, scowling furiously at the forest in the direction from which the blast had come.

The mage who had thrown the energy ball had yet to show himself, but the wolves were on it. Cameron saw several furry shapes converging on the area. He turned to Kaleen, asking without words if she was all right. He was in the middle of the circle casting, but he'd drop everything if she needed him.

"I'm fine," she said when he caught her eye. "Close the circle. We've got work to do."

She probably thought he was going to be inside the circle with her, but after seeing what had just happened, he knew he had decided correctly. He would stay outside and watch her back.

Everything had changed in that instant when he'd seen her go down. He now knew, without a shadow of a doubt, that she was the love of his life. She was his mate. Odd as that might seem for someone of the fey realm. Perhaps he'd been hanging around shifters too long, but whatever the reason, he knew deep in his heart, Kaleen was the only woman who could complete his soul.

His love for Molly had been deep and true, but she had not been meant for him in the end. She had been mortal and meant to go on to other realms without him. Perhaps Kaleen would do the same, but she was at least half-fey, and her dryad side was surely locked to this realm more than any mortal's. He believed she was the one woman meant for him for all eternity. Or however long the Goddess granted them.

He had no idea how it was all going to work out. His family, her family. It was all very complicated—especially when one considered their respective positions in the fey Court—but he would work it out. He had to.

His heart was committed. Seeing her fall had brought home to him how very precious her life was to him. How devastated he would be if she were killed. It all became crystal clear. And way more complicated.

For now, they had a battle to fight, a spell to cast, and a dryad to bring back to the mortal realm and heal. He finished casting the circle, satisfied when it snapped into place with a magical hum. The ladies were protected now, as best he could manage. The spell work would be up to them.

"Cameron!" Kaleen looked at him, her eyes wide as she realized he was outside the ring of protection he had cast. "Why?"

"I'm a fighter, love, and you ladies don't need me to cast the spell. It's dryad magic that's needed, and you have plenty of that." He gave her a smile. He hoped she could read at least some of the confidence in her abilities and the love he felt for her in it. "Now, go on. Get them started."

Chapter Fifteen

A s the only one of the part-dryads with both fey blood and some experience with fey magic, it had been decided that Kaleen would start
and end the spell. Each woman would say her piece and do her bit, but the
power would go around the circle, beginning and ending with Kaleen, who
represented *within*. As such, she had the large quartz crystal and a sprig of willow
leaves in her hands. Leaves from *the* willow. The one Leonora was encased in.

Kaleen looked around and received the agreed-upon nods of readiness that
had been passed around the star. She couldn't see everyone because the tree was
in the way, but they'd decided to pass the ready signal Kaleen's way back when
they'd practiced this in the dining hall. Cameron had drilled them until they all
knew their parts and exactly what to do. Now, they just had to do it.

Kaleen started them off, saying the opening words that would invoke the
spell, and she felt power start to flow weakly through the crystal in her hand.
Next would be Sally, with the carnelian and the athame, followed by Sunny,
with the citrine and lemon peel, and so on down the line until they got back to
Kaleen.

One by one, they said the ritual words, and each time, the power flowing
through Kaleen's crystal leapt a bit in ferocity until, by the end of the seven
points of the star, the power was exponentially greater. Now came another

tricky bit. They'd called the power. Now, they had to use it to get Leonora out of the tree. Once out, they had to direct the power to her healing.

Kaleen looked at the women she could see and nodded. She waited as the nod was passed around the circle, and then, one by one, they all took a step inward, toward the tree, then another, and another. With each step, the circle tightened, the star became more intense, and the power concentrated on the trunk of the willow, which glowed with magic.

Dimly, she became aware of sounds outside the protective circle of salt. They had halted for the moment and were waiting for the signal to begin again. Kaleen had a moment to spare to see what was going on outside the ward and what she saw stirred her anger. The wolves were engaged on multiple fronts, and Cameron had manifested his glowing ethereal armor and was deflecting powerful mage bolts with his magical sword.

The wolf Pack was under attack!

"Wait just a minute!" she shouted so the other women would hear. "I'm going to do something to help our friends outside the ward."

Harnessing her fey energy through her mother's ring, Kaleen cast a spell she had learned at her mother's knee. It was a simple spell for which, her mother had always said, Kaleen had a particular talent. Kaleen had used it as a child for amusement, but right now, it would help things settle down outside the circle so the part-dryads could have a bit of peace in which to work the very important magic they were trying to accomplish.

With a Word of High Fey Magic, Kaleen raised her ringed hand and made everything within two hundred yards of her position freeze. The combatants froze in place. Even the water, animals and insects slowed to an imperceptible crawl as time slowed to a near stop, for a bit, outside the circle of salt. Or maybe it was that time sped up inside the circle. Kaleen didn't know for certain, but either way, this might give them the chance they needed to complete their work without further interference from outside.

"All right. Let's get this show on the road," Kaleen said, turning back to her cousins who were all grinning at her.

Again, she started the chant and the series of movements they would all make toward the tree. This part had been choreographed by Sunny, who had drilled them into a dance-like procession that brought them all closer to the tree step by magical step. Words and motion and stone and branch all had power, coalescing in the center of the star, in the willow itself, this time.

As they moved and watched, spoke their words and made the motions of magical glyphs in the air that glowed with energy, the tree began to split—not physically, but magically. A line of golden-green light opened in the side of the tree, and a glowing forest spirit stepped forth, bathed in the pure light of magic her descendants had called.

They'd done it! At least, part of it. They had more to do as they closed in on the tree and the glowing dryad who was now separate from the tree that had housed her spirit for so long. She was weak, but that could be easily fixed when they had so much magical power gathered in one place. Kaleen nodded once more to her cousins and got the next part of this spell moving.

One by one, they stepped forward and raised their stones high, sending tendrils of the energy concentrated in them toward their ancestor. Seven times, Leonora received an infusion of purified dryad energy gathered using this strongest of fey magical spells. Seven times, Leonora gained strength. By the fourth or fifth infusion, her wounds were gone, and her body was healed. By the end, she was back at full strength—and then some.

Leonora had tears running down her cheeks, but she was smiling so very bright. She smiled at each one of her many-times-great granddaughters, dancing around the tree trunk to see them all. This was a full-blooded dryad, and Kaleen was charmed by her spritely ancestor. She smiled back, but there was still work to do.

"Just one more thing, Grandmother," Kaleen told her quietly, "and then, we can celebrate your return." Kaleen nodded to the others and began the final stage of what they'd planned.

They wouldn't just disperse all this energy with no purpose. No, they were going to create super-strong wards for the Pack territory while they were at it. The Pack had been so good to Leonora over the years, and it had taken in at least three of her descendants as mates. It had befriended all the others. This was the least they could do to repay the Pack's kindness.

Each of the seven had picked their spot and mapped out the territory they would think of while the energy was released. Kaleen, holding the clear stone, would set the ward, and she'd push everyone of evil intent off the mountain while she was at it. She hadn't intended to do anything of the kind when she'd come up with this plan, but now that they were faced with what looked like a full-scale invasion frozen in time just outside their circle of protection, she was adding that to her *to do* list. It should be easy enough, considering that the ward was designed to keep just such people out of the territory altogether.

As she pushed the ward down the mountain, she'd push those bad guys right along with it, leaving the wolves and their allies in place. They could always chase down the bad guys later. Right now, it was important to Kaleen to end the bloodshed and get the bad people out of the territory, once and for all. If her ward worked the way she thought it would, nobody of ill intent would ever be able to cross into Pack territory again.

That was her goal, at least—a permanent ward. Even if she couldn't make it stick forever, they had enough power gathered that whatever ward they managed to put up should last a good long while. Centuries, at the very least. Privately, though, she was hoping it would be permanent.

Setting her intentions, she raised the crystal high, pouring out the power that they had previously poured in, the crystal magnifying the concentrated power held in all the stones, taking in all the colors and purifying them into a single white beam that billowed out and down, seeping out of the salt circle and out over the forest.

As the billowing power moved, it swept up the enemy and tumbled them like grains of sand in an ocean current. Unstoppable power rolling them down the mountain, out of Pack territory, and dumping them on the road below the mountain that was now the edge of the strongest ward Kaleen had ever had the privilege to participate in producing.

When it was done, she lowered her shaking limbs and breathed heavily. She hadn't realized how physically draining it would be to channel that much energy. But she still had a few things to do. With a wave of her hand, she released the wolves and their allies from her freeze spell. Then, she went to the line of salt and brushed away a portion of it with her toe.

When the circle was broken, a rush of energy came into it from the forest around them, like nothing Kaleen had ever experienced. It didn't feel dangerous. It felt more...benevolent, and sort of...divine? She didn't know why she thought that, but the idea remained with her even as she swooned.

Kaleen couldn't quite believe it. She actually swooned for the very first time in her life. The world spun, and she would have fallen, except for the strong arms that came around her, catching her. Cameron, of course.

"Och, lass, you were magnificent," he whispered, gathering her close to his warm body. "Are you all right?"

"Fine," she whispered. "Just really woozy, all of a sudden. Tell the wolves that they might be able to catch the bad guys if they go down to the road."

"They're already on it," Cameron reported back to her. "I think they were enjoying the battle, but you did the right thing. There were a lot more of the enemy than I expected, with a lot more magical firepower. The *Venifucus* is getting ever bolder and sending their really powerful mages out more often now."

"Makes me wonder if their *mater priori* is back," a musical female voice asked from over Kaleen's shoulder.

"She is, according to two mages who met their end trying to stop us from reaching you," Cameron said, perking up and addressing the newcomer. "Good to see you in the flesh, my old friend. Leonora, this is your granddaughter, Kaleen. Kaleen, this is the dryad, Leonora."

Leonora smiled, her green eyes twinkling at Kaleen. "It's a happy day for dryad kind. The Mother of All has blessed your work here, and now, you and your cousins are all full dryads."

"We're... What?" Kaleen shook her head, leaning heavily on Cameron for support. She looked around and saw each of her cousins leaning on their mates, who had rushed to their sides.

Leonora's laugh tinkled through the leaves of the trees, which chattered in happiness to have her back among them. Kaleen heard it in a different way than she always had. The trees seemed even more communicative than they had before. She understood them more completely. It was...strange.

"My mother is fey," Kaleen said, feeling very confused. "Did the Elven Star do something to us?" She looked around at her cousins again, and they all seemed to have a sort of shocked wonder on their faces.

"Your acts of bravery and kindness in using your power to protect the wolves did not go unnoticed. It has been eons since a new dryad has been created. You have just witnessed the activation of *seven* dryads. There are eight of us in this realm now. Enough to do some real good for the planet and its forests." Leonora looked smugly satisfied.

Sally came over and smiled brightly at Leonora. "It's good to see you whole again, Grandmother," she said. "But we're only part-dryads. Our blood is too dilute...right?"

"Not anymore," Leonora said, flinging her arms wide. The whole forest answered her joy with rustlings of its own that spoke louder than words to Kaleen's newly awakened senses.

"This is weird," Maria said, moving closer with the support of her mate, Jesse. "I can hear things I've never heard before. From the trees," she clarified, looking oddly at the forest around them as Leonora chuckled again.

"It will take some getting used to, I have no doubt, but you will have plenty of time in which to do so now. Welcome to the life of an earth elemental, my children. My prayers have been granted, and your courage has been rewarded." Leonora went to hug each and every one of the women who had formed the Elven Star, thanking them each for their willingness to help her out of her predicament.

"I've made sure to keep your house in good order," Sally told Leonora after she'd thanked everyone. "But won't you come up to the Pack house tonight? I'd love a chance to catch up with you, as would everyone else, I think. If you're up to it, that is," Sally added quickly.

"Up to it? After all that magical energy you seven just gave me? I could do cartwheels down the mountain and back up again with all the power flowing through me. I will gladly accept your invitation and would love to spend time getting to know you all better. It's been so long since I had family. I'm just... I'm overwhelmed by all the blessings." Leonora's eyes sparkled with happy tears, and she couldn't speak further, but they all understood.

"Just to be clear," Jesse asked from Maria's side, "you're saying that all seven of these ladies have now become elemental powers in their own right? Like you?"

"Yes." Leonora beamed, looking at them all fondly. "More dryads in the world, especially at this time, is a good thing."

"All are mated to powerful Others," Cameron observed, looking around the group. "They will make formidable teams to fight against the forces of evil."

"They already are," Leonora agreed, nodding. "They just need a bit more training, which I am more than happy to give, as far as being an earth elemental goes. You men will have to teach them the spy-ninja stuff."

Cameron laughed outright at Leonora's words, as did the other men. "I think Jesse and Arlo can work up a training program for the physical stuff," Jason said, only half-joking as he stood next to his detective mate. Sally just elbowed him in the ribs before reaching out to Leonora.

Sally took the dryad's arm, and they walked, together, back to the Pack house, with Jason keeping watch over both of them. Everybody else followed behind, two-by-two. Cameron and Kaleen were the last in the little procession, and she held his hand as she got her bearings. The dizziness had faded, but the sounds of the forest were still extra-sharp in her ears. She was going to have to get used to that, she supposed, if Leonora's words were true.

"What is my mother going to say?" Kaleen wondered aloud, and Cameron chuckled.

"She's probably going to be chuffed. Before you were half-fey and part-dryad. Now, you're full-power dryad, and that trumps just about anything. Even a full fey won't dare mess with a fully functioning elemental power," he told her quietly.

"Seriously?" Kaleen asked him. She couldn't quite believe what he was saying.

Cameron nodded. "Seriously. You're an elemental. That's something incredibly special in any realm, my little sparrow. You outrank practically everyone now, magically speaking. But you're going to have to put in some work to learn everything you can about your new abilities and sensitivities. I suspect your best bet will be to stay near Leonora for the adjustment period, so she can show you the ropes."

"But my house—" she protested, but he cut her off with a kind smile to blunt his words.

"Isn't safe at the moment. The enemy knows where you live. And now that you have a new power, your responsibility is to learn how to use it to the best of your ability."

"I get that," she protested mildly. "I just... I miss my garden," she admitted finally.

"It'll still be there when you get back," he said, stroking her arm in a comforting way. "Maybe you can make a little patch of garden somewhere on the mountain in the meantime or help someone else who has a garden that needs your magic touch."

"It's not quite the same, but those *are* good ideas," she allowed. "I suspect working with plants is going to be one of the things I need to practice again now anyway."

"I suspect you're right."

Cameron was keeping an eye out as they walked along, she knew. Kaleen was in no shape, at the moment, to be wary, though after the placing of that ward and all the magic that had washed through Pack lands tonight, there shouldn't be anything bad left on the mountain. Still, it was comforting to know that she could trust Cameron to always keep her safe. She felt it to the depths of her soul. A sudden thought occurred to her.

"Everything's changed now, hasn't it?"

She stopped walking. They were by the back deck of the Pack house, and the others were disappearing within. Cameron stopped and faced her, his expression understanding.

Chapter Sixteen

"**A**ye. Some things have changed, but not all. For one thing...I still love you. That hasn't changed, and never will." Cameron hadn't really meant to declare himself quite like this, but the moment the words left his lips, he knew it was the right thing to do. He held his breath waiting to see how she would respond.

"You love me?" she whispered, her tone tinged with awe and her eyes lighting with happiness. He began to breathe again, relieved.

"That I do." Cameron paused, thinking through his words. He knew he had to tell her everything so that his past with Molly could never come between them in the future. "I thought I was in love once before. A thousand years ago, I loved a mortal lass named Molly. I lived with her for more than a century, extending her life as best I could. I even gave her a fey mating mark to try to preserve her life with magic from the fey realm." He saw how Kaleen's eyes clouded, but she wasn't rejecting him, so he went on. "I wore that mating mark for a thousand years...until just a few days ago."

"What happened? Did you remove it?" she asked, breathless.

"Such a thing can never be removed by force of will," he told her. "It began to fade after I met you. Each time I kissed you, it grew weaker and paler. And after we made love, it disappeared altogether. That's when I finally understood."

"Understood what?" She searched his eyes and he was powerless to deny her the truth.

"I realized that Molly was never my true mate. She was a lovely part of my past. A beautiful interlude that we both enjoyed, but she could never share her soul with me. Ultimately, we were too different. She died a thousand years ago and I mourned her for a long time. Then, the Goddess made me Her servant, and I found a new reason for living. I've done Her bidding ever since. But since meeting you, little sparrow, I have found a new reason to go on. A reason not to just keep existing, but to look forward to each day and enjoy life again." He smiled at her. "You, Kaleen. You are my reason for living. You are in my heart now, and forevermore."

Kaleen gasped and her eyes sparkled even as a smile lit her lips. He took it as a good sign. Cameron knelt before her, taking one of her hands in his as he looked up into her beautiful face.

"Fey don't always find their perfect mates, the way shifters can, but every once in a while, there is a match destined to happen. I believe we are one of those. I believe Fate drew me to you and has been watching over us. I started to believe that might be the case, but in the moment when that mage blast knocked you down, and I feared the worst for a split-second, I knew I could not go on without you. That's the moment I knew. We were meant to be together, and what I have been feeling all along is pure and true. I love you, Kaleen, and always will."

Tears glistened on her cheeks in the pale light of the moon. She was so beautiful to him. He would remember this moment for the rest of his life. The moment—he hoped and prayed—she would accept his love and give hers and return.

She didn't answer with words at first. She seemed overcome with emotion, and then, Cameron noticed something happening around them. It was only early spring, and most of the plants had not really begun to flower the way they would in full summer, but around them, the night filled with the fragrance of blooms, and as he took a glance around, the forest writhed in happiness. Tendrils of flowering vines were creeping up the posts that held the deck in place, blooming ahead of their time as Kaleen's new powers and strong emotions combined to create a show garden of lovely proportions.

What the wolves were going to think in the morning when they saw this, Cameron didn't know, but that was the last thing he cared about. Right now, his mind was on his lady.

"I think that means you're happy, right?" he asked, standing and gesturing toward the midsummer garden that had sprung up out of nowhere.

"Happier than I can say," she finally answered, hiccupping a little bit through her tears. She turned to him and flung her arms around his neck, hugging him close. "I love you too, Cameron. So much. I didn't dare hope—"

Kaleen didn't seem able to finish the sentence, but Cameron understood what she meant. His heart lifted in joy, just as he lifted her in his arms and carried her onto the deck, and then into the house. Others saw them. Someone else closed the door behind them, but he ignored them all as he walked straight up the stairs with her in his arms, to the suite they had been assigned.

Other people were celebrating. He thought he saw some of the new dryads and their mates gathered in the dining room as he passed the archway, but he wasn't going to stop. He and his love needed to be alone for a while. They needed to settle things between them. He had to tell her more things about himself and his family. They had to speak of the future.

All that could wait until later. Perhaps, much later. First, he was going to set about proving how much he loved her in the most basic way.

Kaleen's heart was floating lighter than air, up above the clouds where happiness lived. Cameron loved her. He'd actually declared himself, and she'd told him the deepest secret of her heart. That she loved him too.

It hardly seemed real, but here he was, carrying her up the stairs and over the threshold of their suite, kicking the door shut behind them. It was like something out of an old movie. Some romantic impulse that literally swept her off her feet.

"I believe that's the human ritual taken care of," Cameron said, putting her down on the bed. "Carrying one's bride across the threshold, I mean."

"Am I your bride?" she asked breathlessly.

Cameron held her gaze and nodded slowly. "As soon as we can arrange the ceremony, if that is your wish. We can be married in the human style, with all the trappings. I always liked wedding feasts in this realm, and now, we have a great number of people to invite."

"We do, don't we?" she said, shocked once again at how much her life had changed in such a short period of time.

"But we can discuss those plans later," he said, his voice dropping low as he joined her on the big bed. "Right now, I've got other plans to work on." He reached for her at the same time she reached for him, both in accord with whatever plan he had in mind.

They undressed each other, eager to be skin to skin. Before too much longer, they had both achieved that first goal. Now, for the rest. He kissed her everywhere as he uncovered each new part of her body. She writhed under his touch, enjoying every moment. When he let her move, she did the same for him, running her hands down his chest and following with her mouth. She kissed his rippling muscles, learning the shape and taste of him as she moved downward.

Cameron tried to stop her when she reached for his hardness, but she would not be denied. She grasped him firmly, then kissed her way downward until she could take him in her mouth and finally discover for herself what it took to make him shiver with need. It made her feel powerful, but she wasn't a tyrant. She would give him what he wanted, in due time.

"You are a temptress, sent to drive me insane," he joked, gasping as his hands tangled in her hair.

Kaleen didn't quite know if he was trying to pull her closer or push her away. Apparently, neither did he. She smiled to herself, feeling triumphant. Finally, she could give him a little of what he'd been giving her. The conflicting emotions, the momentary ecstasies, the whirlwind of feeling and sensation. He was everything she'd ever wanted in a lover, and she wanted to be the same for him.

Finally, he did push her away, gently. Only to turn the tables. He had his wicked way with her, parting her legs and dipping his head to kiss her in the most intimate way. He lingered there until she reached a first completion, but it wasn't anything like what she wanted. She wanted to reach that higher pinnacle with him. Only with him.

But Cameron reared up, resting on his knees and looking at her. She wasn't sure what he was about. She wanted him inside her. This was no time to be playing games. Then again, his games had already proven to be the most fun she'd ever had in a bed...or out of it. She would follow where he led.

"Do you trust me?" he asked, his head tilted as he regarded her, his smile devilish.

"Yes..." Kaleen dragged out the reply, wondering what he had in mind.

His smile widened. "I promise you'll like this. Get on your hands and knees. I want to take you from behind this time. At least to start."

She felt a shiver run through her body at the very thought. They hadn't tried this before, and she found she liked the commanding tone of his voice. She was learning all sorts of new things about herself with him. So far, he hadn't been wrong. She quickly moved into position.

He didn't waste any time but joined himself to her almost immediately, sliding home as if he belonged there. Within her. She thought about it for a moment and thought, perhaps he did. He was, after all, the love of her life. Like the true mate of the shifters or the One of the bloodletters. Cameron was all she would ever desire. The only man she believed had been made expressly for her in all the universe.

He began a fast rhythm, and she was totally on board for whatever he would do. Her excitement level was already high, and she was well on her way to her next orgasm when he slapped her ass, bringing an unexpected edge to their love play. Kaleen yelped, but it hadn't hurt. It had merely surprised her. And excited her.

She would have shaken her head if she'd had energy to spare. As she had thought, Cameron was teaching her all sorts of new things about herself, once again.

Kaleen's muscles tightened in anticipation, and when he tapped her bottom again, she came harder than she ever had before. She felt him join her a moment later as he gripped her hips with strong hands and held her to him as his body spasmed.

He shouted her name, and she moaned his. They came apart and back together in a breathless moment of time where they knew only each other.

She must have blacked out for a bit, because the next thing she knew, she was cuddled in his arms on the bed. He had taken care of her, as he had from the first. Making sure she was comfortable and safe. He was such a good man. The love she felt for him overflowed and followed her into sleep, safe and secure with the man she loved.

When Cameron and Kaleen went down for breakfast the next day, they were both smiling. Kaleen knew they must look silly—or, at the very least, lovestruck—but she couldn't help it. She held his hand as they descended the stairs, unable to be next to him without touching him, now that she had the right to do so. He was hers. He'd told her that over and over last night, until she believed it with every fiber of her being. Just as she was his. No question about it.

"I know I must be grinning like a fool, but I can't seem to help it," she whispered to him as they reached the bottom stair. He turned and leaned in for a quick kiss.

"We have every reason to smile, and these wolves are no stranger to newly mated couples," he said quietly when he lifted his head. "They may tease us a bit, but I don't mind. Do you?"

She shook her head slightly. "No. Not really. I'm so happy and content, not much can bother me right now." She lifted up and gave him another peck on the lips before stepping back. She turned to resume their path toward the dining room, but they'd been caught, well and truly.

Sally and Maria were both standing a few feet away, smiling from ear to ear. It was Maria who spoke first, talking to Sally in a loud voice that carried to Kaleen and Cameron.

"I think I know where that new blooming summer garden by the back deck came from. Weren't they the last two inside last night?"

Sally folded her arms across her chest, grinning. "You know, I think you're right, Maria. And they disappeared upstairs right away, without pausing for the debrief in the dining room. I wonder why they were in such a hurry?"

"Do you two have something to tell us?" Maria challenged in a teasing way.

"We do," Cameron announced, "but first, I must speak with Leonora. Is she here?"

Sally eyed him. "She's on the phone in the office, talking to High Priestess Bettina. She's been in there a while, so she's probably almost done."

"Then I'm afraid any announcement will have to wait," Cameron said, obviously disappointing the two women. "We are fey. Things must be done in a certain way," he explained.

"Well, I'm only half-fey," Kaleen put in, "but if it's important to Cameron to observe all the etiquette, then I'm inclined to humor him." Kaleen winked at her cousins and giggled.

"All right then," Sally said decisively, unfolding her arms, seemingly not taking offense. "Have it your way. The scouts have been reporting in all morning about the new ward and its effectiveness."

"Really?" Kaleen asked, super curious to hear how the magic they'd tried to do last night had settled out. "Is it like we planned?"

Sally smiled drawing out her response. "Even better." She looked appropriately smug, and Kaleen felt joy fill her at Sally's words. She'd wanted to do something good with all that excess energy, and if had worked out even better than they'd hoped, that was fantastic.

"The boys have got a map on the table in the dining room, and they're marking out the shape and location of the ward. It's..." Maria made a face, tilting her head to the side and raising her eyebrows. "It's really impressive."

Kaleen stepped forward. "I want to see," she said simply. Cameron let go of her hand, and when he didn't follow, she turned to look at him.

"I'm going to see if Leonora is free. I really do want to talk with her first."

"Okay," she replied quickly, sensing this was important to him. "Do you want me to come with you?"

"No, I can speak to her alone if you want to look at the map," he said. "It's just a formality, but an important one. Thanks for humoring me. I guess you're going to find out that I'm a bit old fashioned in some respects, and the customs of the fey realm feel right to me when it comes to the important things...like this. When it comes to our relationship, I want to do everything right. As much as possible anyway."

She stepped back and cupped his cheek, drawing him down for a kiss. "This is a two-way street, my love. I'm happy to do whatever you like, as long as we can be together."

"Thank you, little sparrow. I feel the same." He grinned at her as she moved away again.

Cameron went down the back hallway to the office, glad to see the door was open and Leonora was just hanging up the phone. He knocked, and she looked up.

"May I join you?" he asked politely.

"Certainly," Leonora replied, gesturing for him to enter and take the guest chair in front of the desk behind which she was still seated.

"I am pleased you're back among us, milady," he began, not really sure how to broach the subject he needed to discuss.

"I owe you a great deal, Cameron. I've heard how helpful you were with Pam's rescue and then how you took off to find Kaleen before the enemy could get to her. And then, you coached them all through the Elven Star ritual..." She trailed off for a moment. "I scarcely think a simple thank you can suffice, but it is all I have for you at the moment."

"No thanks are necessary, milady," he assured her. "It was my honor to assist. And...I believe Fate stepped in to bring Kaleen and I together, if you believe in such things."

"You know, I've always been a big believer in Fate. Of course, I believe the Fates are guided and directed by the Mother of All, but I suspect you know more about that than I do, since you are one of Her servants." Leonora eyed him knowingly. "How comes a fey knight to be sworn to the service of the Goddess?"

Cameron shrugged. "Oh, the usual way, I suspect. I had lost direction in my life. I wanted to serve, but my family had no real need of my skills. Even if they did, they would have me fight for political intrigues and power plays. That's not what I wanted to do with my life. I wanted to serve a higher cause than petty squabbles in the fey realm. I wanted to make a difference in the eternal battle."

"The eternal battle between good and evil, you mean," Leonora said, nodding. "It is why I remained here in the mortal realm when most of the magic folk fled. I wanted to be part of the solution. Part of the battle against Elspeth the first time she tried her shenanigans here. Looks like—thanks to you and my granddaughters—I'll be here for the second attempt as well."

"If it comes to that, I'm sure the forces of Light will be glad to have your assistance and learn from your experience," Cameron assured her. "But I wanted to ask you something."

"Ask away," she said, leaning back in the chair behind the desk, opening her arms out to the side in a gesture of acceptance.

"Would you have any objection if I told you that I believe Kaleen is the partner Fate decreed for me? In lieu of her father, it is only right that I state my intentions to her next of kin. I wish to marry her and be by her side for all time." He couldn't say it any plainer than that.

"I have absolutely no objection whatsoever, my dear Cameron, but what will your parents say?" Leonora eyed him with an all-too-knowing expression. She knew his parents and knew just who and what they were. She knew the challenges he would face should he take a mate not of the fey realm.

"I would hope they would congratulate me and my beloved. She is, after all, a fey heiress, herself."

"Even if she's only half-fey?" Leonora challenged.

"Ah, but after last night, she is also a powerful earth elemental. I don't think they can object to that sort of energy being introduced into the family line." He shook his head. "My family always lusted for more power, and magic is magic. Elemental magic is something quite different...and rare. They ought to like that," he reasoned. "Besides, I'm far down the line of succession, and I've gone my own way for centuries. They ought to be used to me being unconventional by now."

"Well, if it comes to a struggle with them, you will have my support—as long as being your bride is what Kaleen wants," she added shrewdly.

"Then I have your blessing?" His heart leapt with hope.

She bowed her head. "You do, my boy. I liked you as a lad, and you've grown into a strong man of deep conviction and character. I believe Kaleen's parents would be happy to welcome you into the family, were they here, and since they are not, I will do so in their place." Leonora stood and walked around the desk. Cameron scrambled to stand as the dryad reached out to hug him. "You're a good man, Cameron, and I believe you'll be good to my granddaughter." Leonora released him, and her eyes twinkled up at him as she grinned. "Now, all you have to do is convince her."

"Already done," he replied. "I just wanted to talk to you first before I made the announcement to the Pack. You know how the wolves like to go overboard with the parties." He rolled his eyes in amusement, and Leonora laughed her chime-like chuckle. She looped her arm through his and made a move toward the door.

"Let's go see what the wolves say," she said, still smiling. "I feel just in the mood for a party."

Chapter Seventeen

C ameron spotted Kaleen as soon as he entered the dining room with
Leonora on his arm. They went straight over to where she was standing,
talking with Cece and her mate, Deke. Leonora took Kaleen's hands and smiled
happily at her.

"Congratulations, my dear. When we get your parents back, I'm sure they'll
agree with your selection, but for now, I have given my blessing. You couldn't
find a better man than Cameron. Even if his family is a bit...touchy," Leonora
said, tilting her head to one side.

"What's this?" Cece asked, an interested light in her eyes.

Leonora stepped back, releasing Kaleen's hands, and Cameron moved closer,
putting one arm around Kaleen's waist. Staking his claim. He felt almost smugly
happy that they were now officially a couple.

"Kaleen has consented to be my bride," Cameron told everyone within
earshot. Most of the dryads and their mates were in the immediate vicinity and
turned around to offer their congratulations.

Whatever they had been discussing previously was put aside while everyone
came over to speak to the happy couple. Jason made some sort of signal to
those of his Pack who ran the kitchen, and within moments, a breakfast feast
began to appear on the sideboards as more and more of the Pack arrived to get

the festivities started. It looked like they were going to have an old-fashioned wedding breakfast, though it was a bit non-traditional in scope.

"How did you organize this so fast?" Cameron asked Jason a little while later as they watched the children of the Pack playing games to one side of the big room. This was an all-out Pack gathering that Cameron hadn't quite expected so quickly.

"Well, I had an inkling when Sally mentioned the sudden appearance of a summer garden out by the deck this morning. She began to speculate, and I thought a little get-together would be good for the Pack anyway, after everything that's happened. We also wanted to celebrate the new wards that the ladies managed to set around our territory. I went out and took a look at them earlier, and it's purely amazing. That kind of protection is a game changer for us. The whole Pack wanted to thank the dryads for giving us such an incredible gift." Jason gestured around the room which was filled to capacity with members of the wolf Pack. "I let it be known that today was a holiday, and that if people wanted to gather here and thank our benefactors, they should bring the family for a day of togetherness. The fact that we can also celebrate a new mating at the same time is a happy bonus."

"Well, however it happened, I appreciate your including us in your celebration. My parents never leave the fey realm, and Kaleen's parents are stuck there as well. Right now, our circle is rather small, and I wanted her to be able to feel the joy of our pairing. It's not quite the same for us as it is for you shifters, but I believe Kaleen is the woman Fate made just for me, and vice versa. That is something rare and special among the fey, and I'd hate to let such an occasion pass without marking it in some way. Thanks for letting us do that here."

Jason slapped Cameron on the back in a friendly way. "Happy to help, my friend. You are, after all, part of the family now. You're Pack, whether you realized it or not. Our mates are cousins, which makes you part of my family. My Pack."

Cameron just shook his head as he smiled. "I never expected to be part of a wolf Pack, but if that's what Fate has sent us, then who am I to argue?"

A while later, Cameron and Kaleen were sitting together at a table with several of the other dryads when Leonora joined them. She sat next to Kaleen and patted her hand.

"Now then, we need to work on getting your parents back from the fey realm," she announced. "Sir Cameron, can you help with that or is it something we dryads can do on our own?" She punctuated her words by taking a big bite out of an apple turnover.

Kaleen was nonplussed by Leonora's casual words. Kaleen didn't think there was any easy way to cross between the realms, but Cameron had done it, she realized suddenly. So had her mother. There had to be a way. Maybe it wasn't as impossible as she'd always thought.

Cameron took Kaleen's hand reassuringly but addressed his words to Leonora.

"As you know, going Between is never done lightly. I have not been back to the fey realm for a very long time as the mortal realm reckons years, but I would like my family to know about Kaleen, and I would like to discover what's happened to Kaleen's parents as well. If we can do both things at once, so much the better, but it will require a great deal of magical power. I can perform the spell, but I will need you and your granddaughters to help power it," Cameron said.

For the first time in a long time, Kaleen felt her hopes rise in regard to seeing her parents again.

"Do you really think we can do it?" Kaleen asked Cameron, clutching at his arm.

Cameron took her right hand from his arm and fingered the ring on her finger. Her mother's ring. One of *the* rings of power.

"With the aid of this little trinket, it is more than possible," he told her. "And with your cousins at your side, I don't think anyone would dare deny you the right to retrieve your parents from anything they might be doing in the fey realm. As it happens, I believe I know a little about your mother's family. She is the rightful heir to one of the royal lines, and this ring is her birthright. Knowing what I know of the rest of her family, I suspect what they really want is the ring, but I don't propose that you give it to them. It has been passed—and rightly so—to you, and it is now yours to do with as you will. You make your home here in the mortal realm. We are currently—or will likely soon be—under attack by Elspeth and her followers. You will need this ring to fight them off, and I think you would be well within your rights to keep it. With Elspeth on the horizon, you have more need of it than anyone in the fey realm."

"But what if they want me to trade the ring for my parents?" Kaleen would give almost anything to have her parents back.

"They likely will ask exactly that, but I believe you should not give in. You outrank everyone simply by your birth, even if you are only half-fey. You are now a full-powered earth elemental. Even in the fey realm, that counts for a lot. Only the King and Queen rank higher than you, my love. You can rightfully demand the return of your parents without giving up your birthright." He kissed her hand before releasing it and putting his arm around her waist, snugging her close to his side. "And besides, I will be with you. I dare anyone to try to force you to do anything. It will be my pleasure to impress upon them the error of their thinking."

Kaleen thought about that. Cameron was a fey knight. A sworn servant of the Goddess. She had no doubt about his prowess. He would protect her both physically and magically.

"And if anybody gives you trouble," Leonora put in with a cunning wink at Cameron, "your new mate outranks everyone but his own parents, the monarchs of the fey realm."

"Wait. What?" Kaleen wasn't certain she'd heard that correctly. It really sounded as if Leonora had just said that Cameron was some kind of fey prince.

"We haven't had a lot of time to talk about this, but I am, indeed, a younger son, so far down the line to inherit that it will never happen. I chose my own path, and nobody objected. In fact, my parents are proud that I was called to the service of the Goddess. But the fact remains that, yes, I am—or was—a prince in the fey realm. But you, my love, are a duchess. We're not so far apart in status there, though none of that matters, really. The only thing that matters is the here and now and how much we love each other."

She felt the truth of his words down to her soul, but she couldn't help but think about the fact that he was royalty. She was marrying a prince. Like some kind of fairytale. Only this was a *real faerie* tale.

"Well, I always thought you were a prince of a guy, coming to our rescue," Pam said with blatant humor. "I just never realized you actually were a prince. Your Highness."

Cameron held up one hand, palm outward, even as he grinned and shook his head. "Let's not start with that. I've loved living here in the mortal realm because I've been able to just be me and be judged on my own merits. I didn't ask to be born to that family, and I never really cared much about being royal. Let's just forget all that, can't we?"

Pam chuckled. "Not sure if I can actually forget it, but I can definitely lay off the teasing. After all, you're going to be my cousin by marriage. We're family."

"You can forget all the royal falderal, young Cameron, but not quite yet. First, you have to use your position, your power and your skill to retrieve Kaleen's parents. Once you've accomplished that, you can do whatever you want regarding your titles," Leonora reminded him.

"Yes, milady," he answered, bowing his head to her in respect. "You definitely have a point. We'll need to come on strong and use every weapon in our arsenal to make a show the fey will respect."

"When can we do this?" Kaleen asked him, feeling anxious. "Will we have to wait long?"

Cameron shook his head slowly. "We can do it whenever your cousins are ready, actually. Might as well act now while everybody is gathered in one place."

"Tonight," Leonora intoned, and everyone listened. "We'll gather by the willow and open a portal. You two will go Between and make the demand. The rest of us will stand watch just outside where they can sense us and perhaps see our power. That ought to be show enough to get some response," Leonora judged, smiling in a cunning way.

"I like your plan, milady," Cameron replied, nodding. "We will do as you say."

That night, after a day spent mostly enjoying the company of the Pack and eating scrumptious food, Kaleen and Cameron went down to the willow with

Leonora and all the other dryads. Their mates came with them as well. All in all, they made a large circle—very similar to what they'd done for the Elven Star, but not quite so elaborate—but the ladies chose to stand at their star points and their mates stood with them.

Leonora took the point where Kaleen had stood the night before. She raised one hand, and some of the pliable young branches to the right of the trunk formed an oval tall and wide enough for Kaleen and Cameron to walk through.

"I've made a suitable anchor," Leonora said, turning to smile kindly at Cameron. "Now, it's your turn to call the portal. We will supply any extra power you might need through our connection with Kaleen."

Cameron nodded at the elder dryad. "Thank you, milady. I haven't done this in quite some time, and never without a divine boost of energy."

Kaleen sensed he was a tiny bit nervous. She took his hand and squeezed it, offering silent support.

"Go get them back," Leonora said quietly, urging them toward the oval she had coaxed into existence.

Cameron nodded once more and turned with Kaleen, not letting go of her hand, to walk to the oval formed by the willow's branches. Since the night before, Kaleen sensed, the tree itself had become infused with magical energy. She suspected that would help with whatever Cameron had to do to make the bridge Between the mortal realm and the fey.

They walked to the oval and stopped, still holding hands. Everyone around them sort of faded into the distance so it felt like it was just Kaleen and Cameron, standing before something big.

"Can I help?" she whispered to him, wanting to ease his burden if she could.

"I couldn't do this without you. Just stay with me, no matter what happens." He turned his head to look at her, and their eyes met and held.

"Always," she told him, meaning it with every fiber of her being.

The moment stretched, but the shifting of the leaves in a sudden breeze reminded them both that they'd come here to do something important. Cameron turned to face the empty ring of twisted and braided willow limbs with a determined expression on his face.

He closed his eyes and bowed his head, breathing deep before he began. Opening his eyes and looking into the center of the oval, he began to speak words that didn't quite register to her ears, though she felt the impact of them with her newly awakened magical senses. She felt the tree quiver in response to the new demands on its magic. A moment later, she felt Cameron pulling on her own magic and the link to her family feeding her more and more power.

A swirling pattern began in the center of the oval hanging, seemingly, in mid-air. It swirled and expanded, becoming ever larger. It was all the colors of the rainbow on a field of stars, sparkling and rotating until it filled the entire oval defined by the willow branches.

Cameron stopped chanting and the portal steadied. He squeezed her hand to get her attention. She looked up at him, the light of the portal painting his beloved face in stained-glass hues.

"Ready?" he asked.

She nodded slowly. "As I'll ever be."

"Just remember to hang on to me and don't leave the Between space or we'll be stuck in the fey realm, and time will pass rapidly here before we can work our way back," he warned.

She hadn't really considered that, but his caution was a good reminder. He knew what they might encounter a lot better than she did. He'd been born and raised in the fey realm, after all. She'd only heard stories and not really good ones. Her mother hadn't ever wanted to go back to the place of her birth. She'd planned to stay in the mortal realm for the rest of her days, but Fate, it seemed—and her family—had had other plans.

Keeping that firmly in mind, Kaleen stepped with Cameron through the portal into the space Between realms.

Chapter Eighteen

It was unlike anything Kaleen had ever seen before. Unlike any place she'd ever been before. The light was bright white, tinged with all those rainbow colors swirling behind them and off in the distance, but where they stopped, just inside their own portal, everything was stark white, bright and sort of misty. She sensed the existence of multiple—perhaps an infinite number—of places they could go from here, but Cameron didn't move a step farther.

"Now, we wait. This energy flux will not go unnoticed, and a Guardian should come," Cameron told her.

"Are there other portals in the distance?" she had to ask but found she couldn't speak above a whisper.

"Yes, many," Cameron confirmed. "But we are closest to the fey realm here. And there are several places we could go from here that would lead to different parts of that realm. I chose the one closest to my home because I know the royal portal is constantly monitored, and we should get the quickest response. Also, your family's lands are not far from the royal estate, and this is probably the closest place I know without having detailed knowledge of your family's holdings. It is likely there is a portal on their lands as well, since your mother went across to the mortal realm and her family was able to snatch your father as well. That argues for something close to home that they've been using when they can scrounge up enough energy to do so. Although portals are known and somewhat common, they are seldom used because of the power requirements. Also, there has to be a compelling reason to go traipsing off to another realm. Usually, there isn't." He shrugged. "Despite the long history of fey in the mortal realm, most of my people never leave home."

"Is that..." She squinted at something in the distance.

"Someone's coming," he said a split second later. "Should be a Guardian. With any luck, it'll be someone I know."

The figure moved closer, taking shape from the mist as it approached with unnatural speed, though it seemed to be walking slowly. It was a man. His tunic was white, embroidered with gold. He wore brown pants and high boots of gleaming black. There was a circlet of gold upon his brow, and his hair was flowing gold with red highlights.

"Cameron? Is that you?" He stopped a short distance from them. "Why do you not come all the way home? And who is that with you?"

"I cannot yet return to the fey realm, but I have news and a request," Cameron stated firmly. "First, I must tell you that Elspeth is likely back in the mortal realm, and her minions have already begun attacking magical folk."

The other man's blond brows drew together in concern. "Go on," he prompted, listening intently.

"But She whom I serve has seen fit to aid the forces of Light. This is Kaleen, a newly minted dryad of full power. She and her six cousins performed the Elven Star rite last night to save the dryad Leonora's life and restore her to the mortal realm. In so doing, the Mother of All blessed the seven descendants of Leonora with full dryad powers."

"It is good to meet you, Dryad Kaleen. I have long known Leonora and count her as a friend," the man replied, nodding slightly to Kaleen. He seemed to pause, taking a closer look at her. "But you are not all earth-born, I sense."

"No, sir. My mother is fey. My father's blood held the dryad lineage," Kaleen spoke for the first time, finding her courage. This man was very intimidating, but at least he was listening. "I came here to ask for the return of them both. My father was snatched away from the mortal realm when I was a child, by my mother's family. She waited until I was grown to go after him and has not been seen since. Many years have passed in the mortal realm while I waited for some news of them both. I come now to ask for their safe return. They do not belong here, and I need them. The forces of Light need them."

The man's frown grew deeper. "Who is your mother? What is her name?"

"My father is Timothy Fairchild. My mother's name is Jilial," she responded.

"Jilial? Has she no surname?" the man asked.

Cameron surprised her by raising their clasped hands and turning hers so that her ring showed to the man.

"This ring was her mother's," Cameron said quietly but firmly. "I have no doubt that her mother is Lady Jilial, Duchess of Eriwande. Wasn't she missing mysteriously from the High Court for a very long time?"

Realization dawned on the other man's face. Then, he seemed to grow angry. "She is still missing, as a matter of fact. Her uncle stands in her place, claiming she is ill and not much enamored of court life."

"I would say she is being held prisoner along with her husband, somewhere on her own estate, by her own family. I believe her uncle wants the ring, but Lady Jilial was wise enough to give it to her heir before she undertook the journey Between to retrieve her mate," Cameron conjectured. The other man seemed to be listening intently.

He paused a moment, then seemed to come to a decision. Out of nowhere, a long wooden staff crowned with a golden orb appeared in his hand. The wood was from a rowan tree, Kaleen could tell with her newly enhanced dryad abilities. The rowan was a very magical and sacred tree, indeed.

The man lifted the staff and brought the end down on the floor of the space Between, making a thudding sound that echoed with more strength than she would have expected. Kaleen had no doubt in her mind that it had been some sort of summoning.

A new man appeared out of the mist, seeming surprised to find himself there. He saw the blond man and bowed, then looked around and saw Cameron.

"Prince Cameron," the man sputtered, "it is good to see you, if a bit strange to be in this place." The man looked around at the misty whiteness and seemed confused.

"Do you not recognize the Between, Lord Eriwande?" Cameron asked.

Kaleen tried not to jump. First, at hearing Cameron called Prince, and second at realizing the name this man carried meant he was probably a relative of hers. Most probably, based on the earlier exchange between the men, this was her mother's uncle.

He was handsome. Tall, lithe, with high cheekbones and angular features. He looked a little bit like her mother, though his expression was harsher than her mother's had ever been. Even when she'd been mad.

"If you are my mother's uncle, then I have a grievance with you, sir," Kaleen said, feeling bold. Her anger was about to boil over, but she kept a tight rein on it. It wouldn't do to lose her temper with these people, who probably already thought humans were uncivilized heathens.

"You have no standing to question me, young lady. I am a Lord of the fey realm. You are human." The man practically spat the last word. It was pretty clear what he thought of humans.

"I am half-fey," she corrected him. "And a dryad." That seemed to get his attention. The man's eyes widened. "Look behind me through the portal, *my lord*. I am not alone. There are seven other dryad earth elementals who back me up in this request. Give my mother and father back, and you can do whatever political machinations you wish in the fey realm. We have a war to fight against Elspeth in the mortal one, and we don't have time for your games."

"Elspeth?" Now, the man looked a little scared if Kaleen was any judge, but he did look over her shoulder, and she could feel the presence of her cousins, as he must also.

"I will give you the man and my niece, but I want the ring of power," the man finally said. "Such a magical artifact does not belong in the mortal realm."

"You want my mother's ring?" Kaleen asked, as if the thought had never occurred to her, though of course, they'd already talked about it. No way was this conniving bastard getting her ring.

"It is a family heirloom. She had no right to hide it from me," Lord Eriwande claimed. Cameron and the Guardian, Kaleen noticed, were both watching with raised eyebrows, though they said nothing.

"You're wrong. The ring was my mother's. It passes to the heir directly. It is not for just anyone in the family to wield. In fact, my mother gave it to me when she went to rescue my father. It is mine now, and you shall not have it." Gosh. She was even beginning to talk like these stuffed shirts. "The fact is, the ring is mine, and it will go to my child when I give it to him or her. It will never be yours. *Can* never be yours. It does not belong in your direct line and never has. Furthermore, I need it. If I have to fight Elspeth, you can bet I'll need all the magic I can get. If all you want it for is prestige and power, then you're barking up the wrong tree, buddy."

He looked confused for a moment, then the intent of her colloquialism impacted, and he grew angry instead. Steam practically came out of his ears, but she could see that he tried to dial it back in front of Cameron and the Guardian.

"If you will not give me the ring, then I will not free your parents," he finally said in a rush.

That's when the Guardian stepped forward. "So, you admit you have them confined?"

Ooh, the lord looked like he just realized he'd made a big mistake admitting that. Good. Let the truth come out. It was about time.

"They are merely guests," Eriwande tried to backpedal.

"Then why have neither of them been seen at Court? The Duchess should have been attending the High Court. She has been asked for repeatedly, but you kept saying she was disinclined to appear. Is it that you have her held prisoner on her own estate? And her mortal mate as well?" The Guardian shook his head. "You know this is against our law. Mortals cannot live here for long, if at all. The time differential is too great, and they have regrets. The law was made to protect them, and you seem to have flouted it in abducting this man away from his family. And not just a man, but a man with elemental blood. For shame, Eriwande. You will be brought up on charges over this, have no doubt."

"But, my liege—"

At that appellation, Kaleen began to get an idea of just who the Guardian was. This was the King of the Fey... Cameron's father. Oh, boy.

The King raised the rowan staff and brought it down. A moment later, Eriwande disappeared.

"I have sent him to the dungeons. He will not escape," the King assured them. "Now, my dear, I must apologize. I had no idea Eriwande was holding his niece and her mate prisoner. He's been very good about keeping up appearances. Please accept my apology. I will summon your parents shortly, but first..." he turned to Cameron, "I just want a moment to say it's good to see you, Cameron. We have missed you, but I know you are doing good work in service of the Mother of All, and we're very proud of that, and of you."

"Thank you, Father." Cameron seemed a bit choked up, and his pale cheeks had a bit of color to them.

The King looked down at their clasped hands and then back up, one eyebrow raised. "Have you something else to tell me, son?"

"Sire, in the course of freeing Leonora and fighting off the *Venifucus*, it's become clear that Kaleen is my fated mate. I have already received Leonora's blessing in lieu of her parents, but I would ask for yours as well."

The King looked at them, a smile reaching his eyes slowly. The moment seemed to draw out as he considered.

"I confess to being very impressed by Lady Kaleen and her relatives that I can just sense beyond your portal. There is great power there, but of course, that is but one consideration in a match that will stand the test of time. Do you love each other?" the King asked.

"I love her," Cameron stated, looking at her. She met his gaze and replied.

"I love you, too."

The King cleared his throat when the silence lengthened, and Kaleen startled and moved her gaze back to the fey King. He was smiling fully now, grinning from ear to ear.

"That is the most important ingredient to a happy marriage," he said. "Your mother will be thrilled, and I hereby give you my formal blessing." The King looked at Kaleen and smiled. "I look forward to getting to know you better in the future, Lady Kaleen." The King then addressed his son directly. "I know you are pledged to serve in the mortal realm for the time being, but when Elspeth is defeated once more, I hope you will spend some time here with us, so we can get to know our new daughter-in-law, and she can get to know us. I believe Kaleen might also enjoy learning more of her ancestral lands, since she is still the only heir to the Eriwande duchy."

"I believe my mother wanted her younger brother to fill the role of Duke," Kaleen offered. "If such a thing is allowable."

"Your mother's uncle was filling in for her, but now that he will be punished for his crimes, it is very natural for her brother to take up the reins," the King told her. "I will make sure he is invested without delay. For now, let us bring this matter to a close, since I know this is costing you all dearly in magical energy." He raised his rowan staff and banged it down again, and as the echo faded, Kaleen saw two people walking hand in hand, out of the mist. They looked perplexed at first, but then, they saw who had summoned them.

"Your Majesty!" Jilial greeted the King first, offering a deep and graceful curtsey, though her eyes were drawn to her daughter.

Kaleen's mother didn't look a day older than when she'd left. Her father, too, looked about the same age as the last time she'd seen him, all those many years ago. He bowed to the King and looked around at the others with a curious gaze that lingered on Kaleen. He squinted as if he wasn't sure what he was seeing.

"My apologies, Duchess Jilial," the King said. "I was only just made aware that you and your mate had been held captive by your uncle. He is in the dungeon, awaiting sentencing. Your brother will be invested post-haste, and you both are free to return to the mortal realm, if that is your wish, with your daughter." The King gestured toward Kaleen. "She has braved the perils of this place to get you both back. She is a brave and powerful woman."

The King winked at Kaleen, and she felt her face heat with a blush.

"But the portal is draining them," the King went on. "Go now and tell your tales on the other side. We are family now, Jilial. You can always come to me if you need help. Rely on that."

The King tapped his rowan staff down once more, and they were all pushed through the portal behind Kaleen and Cameron. The swirling colors dissipated with an audible snap as the portal closed, and all four of them stood under the willow tree, the dryads and their mates around them in the dark of the night. In Wyoming. Not the fey realm. Thank the Goddess.

And suddenly, Kaleen felt really, really tired.

"What did he mean that we're family now?"

Jilial's voice came to Kaleen through the fatigue weighing her limbs. She leaned heavily against Cameron, and his strength supported her, though he was probably just as weary as she was from the energy drain.

"Duchess Eriwande, I am Cameron, youngest son of Liandra and Berwid, sworn to the Goddess to serve in the mortal realm." Cameron was swaying only a little on his feet as he faced her parents. She really needed to get a handle on herself and say something.

Chapter Nineteen

"**M**om? Dad?" Kaleen managed to say, letting go of Cameron's arm to reach out to them. That's all it took for her parents to rush forward and enfold her in a big hug.

It felt so good. She was safe. They were safe. They were all together again. Just as she'd hoped.

Except...

She was in love with Cameron now. And she was a woman grown. It would never be like it had been when she was a child. Those days had been lost to the machinations of her mother's uncle and the time differential of the fey realm. She drew back from them, reaching one hand out for Cameron's.

"Mom, Dad, this is Cameron. He's...uh..." She'd never had to introduce a boyfriend to her parents before, much less the man she was going to spend the rest of her life with. She wasn't sure what to say.

"Milady, milord, I am in love with your daughter, and we plan to be married. Since you were not here, I asked the blessing of your ancestor, sir. The dryad Leonora gave her blessing to our union in your absence. Now that you're both here, I would ask your blessing as well, though I suspect now is not the ideal time." Cameron was standing tall, but Kaleen could tell he was tired. Probably as fatigued as she was, just hiding it better.

"Now is definitely *not* the time," Leonora said, coming closer. She addressed Kaleen's father. "I am Leonora, your many-times-great-grandmother. It is my dryad magic that runs through your veins and has been passed down to your daughter and all the women you see gathered here, who helped provide the magical power to send Kaleen and Cameron Between and bring you back." Leonora shook her head. "But that is not important right this minute. You are in Wyoming, on lands belonging to a strong werewolf Pack. Three of my granddaughters are mated into the Pack, as a matter of fact, and Sally there," she pointed to Sally, who waved tiredly as she leaned against her mate, "is the Alpha female. The handsome young man with her is the Alpha."

"Werewolves?" Timothy Fairchild asked, clearly surprised by the idea.

"Of course, grandson. You just spent years in the fey realm. Surely, you know by now that all sorts of magical creatures not only exist but thrive in the mortal realm." Leonora's tone wasn't unfriendly, but a bit chiding, all the same. "As it happens, we've all been staying at the Pack house, and I, for one, have been very grateful for the Pack's hospitality. I propose we all go back to the house where we can sit and refresh ourselves while we talk over everything that's happened. There's a lot to catch up on."

"An excellent idea," Jason said from the other side of the loose circle that was starting to break up. "You're very welcome at the Pack house, Mr. and Mrs. Fairchild," he called as he turned to walk back, supporting his mate with one arm around her waist.

"Thank you, Alpha," Jilial called back. A fey duchess, she likely knew the importance of being polite to other magical creatures, Kaleen realized.

She and Cameron walked with her parents, headed for the Pack house. Leonora went ahead while they walked more slowly, chatting sporadically.

"What year is it?" Jilial asked.

Kaleen told her and heard her father's quick inhalation.

"So many years?" he muttered in dismay, then spoke more loudly. "I swear, it only felt like a few months, at most. When they took me, you were just a little girl, Kaleen." His voice broke with emotion. "I missed your growing up."

"It's all right, Dad. We have plenty of time to catch up." She reached out to touch his arm, and he took her hand and squeezed it.

"It was only a few weeks for me in the fey realm, but you went from teenager to grownup without me being here," Jilial said, sounding a bit lost. "I mean, I thought it might happen, but I'm not happy about it."

"I wasn't either, but I got used to it, and I don't begrudge it—especially now that I understand about being in love. You went there to help Dad. I get that."

"And it turned out that he didn't really need my help all that much anyway," Jilial said, rolling her eyes. "I mean, I knew there was something magical about Tim when I married him," she put her arm through his and smiled up at him, still obviously very much in love, "but I didn't realize he had elemental power."

"Your magic developed more when you crossed Between," Cameron suggested, and Tim nodded.

"I'd always had a way with gardens and trees, but when they dragged me into the fey realm, my power rose to the surface, and they couldn't keep me imprisoned no matter how hard they tried. The stone of the dungeon was no barrier. The rocks and dirt answered to me, as did the plants and trees. Eventually, they let me have the run of the estate, and I even helped out a little, because even though Uncle Eriwande is a jerk, Jilial's brother is a nice kid. He's trying hard to come out from under his uncle's thumb, but he's young, and the uncle has a lot of loyal retainers who seem blind to his dishonesty." Tim shook his head. "I gained a lot of magical power in my travels, but I didn't have enough—or the knowledge—to get back here."

"I thought I could convince my uncle to let us go, but he was being stubborn. He wanted the ring," Jilial said, anger and disappointment mixed in her voice, "but since I gave it to you, Kaleen, it was no longer mine to give. Thank goodness. I would not have wanted him to have that kind of power."

"What does the ring do?" Tim asked as they walked slowly along.

"Not as much here as it can do there," Jilial answered. "It is a conduit for fey power, and only one of my line can wield it. That's why I gave it to Kaleen," she told her husband quietly. "It is her birthright, even if she never lives in the fey realm."

"But she's going to visit after Elspeth is defeated. Will she be in danger from people wanting to take the ring from her?" Tim asked, worry edging his tone.

"No," Cameron answered with surety. "It is hers and hers alone, and until she passes it to her heir, it will answer to no one else."

Kaleen realized he was talking about a child they might have together, and her heart melted just a little. She hadn't thought about it before, but now the idea of a little girl with Cameron's vivid red hair or a little boy who would grow up to be a man of Cameron's stature... Well, it choked her up, just a little. She couldn't wait to see how things would work out.

"So, you're Prince Cameron," Jilial said after the silence had dragged a bit. "I remember when you were born, but I left the fey realm and never looked back until Uncle abducted my husband." She made a face. "I was friendly with your mother. She is a lovely lady, and your father has always been a just and noble King. I'm relieved he finally has incontrovertible evidence against my uncle. I know the King will live up to his word and take care of my little brother. He's been under my uncle's shadow for far too long."

"My father is as good as his word, and he'll help your brother," Cameron promised. They walked in silence a few more paces before Tim spoke again.

"How did you know my power came out when I traveled Between?" he asked.

Cameron shrugged. "Your last name is a big clue."

"Fairchild? Why is that a clue?" Tim insisted.

"It is one of the many names given, in olden times, to the children of fey and mortal matings. Somewhere, way back in your ancestry, I wouldn't be surprised to find a fey warrior who dallied with a human maid. The blood is very weak in you, but it likely interacted with your dryad blood, and traveling Between would act as a spark to fan the flames of your latent magic to life."

"You don't say." Kaleen's father looked nonplussed as they strolled along. Even Jilial looked surprised.

"I always said there was more to you than met the eye, Tim," Jilial said, snuggling close to her mostly human mate.

"And I never really believed you," he replied easily. "I always felt so surprised that you agreed to be my wife. Flattered. Humbled. And so much in love I couldn't really contain it."

They stopped walking, and she turned to him, reaching up to move her mouth closer to his. "I love you too."

They kissed, and Kaleen smiled, walking slowly, arm in arm with her own mate.

She understood about that kind of timeless love now that she had Cameron in her life. She wondered if years from now they would be like her parents—still very much in love with each other. She thought she knew the answer. Her love for him was a constant, and she felt the same intensity coming from him in her direction. There was little doubt in her mind that they would be every bit as in love a hundred years from now as they were at this moment.

They slowed their pace even more to allow time for Kaleen's parents to catch up. When they did, they resumed their conversation, but everyone was mellow with fatigue and satisfaction at a job well done. Kaleen felt happiness down deep in her core. She had her parents back. Leonora had been rescued and restored as well. And, most importantly, she had Cameron in her life. Things couldn't get much better than this.

"What a lovely garden," Jilial said as they neared the back deck to the Pack house where Kaleen's blooms were still going strong. "Is this your doing?"

Kaleen felt the blush in her cheeks. "This is the result of Cameron asking me to marry him," she admitted. "I didn't really do it on purpose."

Tim chuckled. "I can see how happy his proposal made you if this is the result." He cast a speculative gaze over Cameron. "We'll have to talk more when we've both recovered from this ordeal. I want to get to know the man who could make my daughter so joyful that this—" he gestured to the riot of flowers and greenery all around the back of the deck "—is the result."

They all mounted the steps of the deck, and Leonora was waiting at the back door for them. She smiled at the four of them and touched Tim's hand.

"I never had a son," the ancient dryad said. "Only my daughter, Marisol, who also had girls. Mostly, the dryad power seems to produce girls." She shrugged. "I hope you won't mind, but I'm fascinated by the idea of having a many-times-great-grandson."

"Not at all," Tim said smoothly, his deep voice warm. "I'm fascinated to learn where my way with the earth and growing things came from. I hope we can get to know each other better."

"Absolutely." Leonora beamed as she led the way into the Pack house.

There was a low murmur of sound that could be heard even at the back of the house that grew louder as they approached the front and the arched entrance to the dining hall.

Everyone had gathered there, and food was being served. Snacks and sandwiches to revive those who had used a great deal of their own magic. The wolves were great about having food available for the Pack mates pretty much around the clock, since they had such high metabolisms. They were gracious hosts as well and had welcomed the newcomers as warmly as anyone could wish. It was easy, since three of their Pack had mated three of Leonora's descendants, and the Pack had only grown stronger as a result. All of the dryads were considered part of the extended family now. Part of the extended Pack.

Everyone sat together, and they did a mission debrief right then and there. Hanging around with the shifter soldiers had allowed Kaleen to pick up on some of their lingo. She noted how they were all listening closely to her parents' account of what had happened to trap them in the fey realm and how they'd felt the King's summons that dragged them into that Between space.

They accepted Kaleen's thanks for their help and her parents' gratitude as well. There was a lot of grateful words being exchanged, even as they ate to help replenish their spent energies. Kaleen sat quietly with Cameron next to her, enjoying every minute of the conversation. She just liked watching her folks. Seeing them for the first time in years. Together and still very much in love. It was a minor miracle and a major cause for joy.

She hated the fact that she was going to have to break some very bad news to her father, but he needed to know that Pam was his niece and that his sister had died years ago. As the gathering was beginning to break up, Kaleen gestured to Pam and she nodded, moving off to one side with her mate.

"Dad, there's no easy way to say this," Kaleen started as they joined Pam and Arlo. "Pam is your niece, and her mom died a while back."

Tim's expression went from joy to sorrow as he looked at Pam. "You look a lot like her," he finally said, "and I'm glad to meet you. I'm only sorry I wasn't here when she died. I loved my little sister, though she was a lot younger than me."

Pam hugged her uncle, and they shared a long moment of mutual grief, after which Pam and Tim spoke quietly about the loss of Pam's mother as their mates supported them. Kaleen and her mother watched with sympathy as the others went on their way toward their own beds. Nobody disturbed the family, but a few of the men sent nods to Cameron, which he acknowledged. It was Sally who finally came over to them.

"We have rooms prepared for you," Sally told Tim and Jilial quietly. "Whenever you're ready I can show you to your suite," she offered.

Everybody else was mostly gone. Those that were staying at the Pack house had already headed for the stairs, saying goodnight to those who lived elsewhere on the mountain. They would all reconvene in the morning for breakfast together in the dining room.

Kaleen's little group paused by the door to say goodnight to Pam and Arlo with the promise of talking more the next day. Then, Kaleen and Cameron, as well as Tim and Jilial, mounted the stairs with Sally in the lead.

Kaleen bid her parents good night as Sally led them off to another part of the large house, and she and Cameron went to the end of the hall and their suite. When they reached the privacy of their own room, Kaleen stepped into Cameron's embrace and just hugged him for a long moment, burying her head against his chest.

"Thank you," she whispered. "Thank you for everything. I was so afraid I'd never see them again."

Her emotions threatened to overwhelm her as she clung to him. He stroked her back with his big, strong hands and just held her, making soothing sounds.

"There now, little sparrow. It's all done now. We've saved Leonora, and now, we have your family back together. I'd call that a job well done."

"It is. And I'm so happy I could burst," she replied, leaning back to look up into his beloved face. "I'm just... A little overwhelmed is the best way to describe it, I guess."

His expression changed, and he lifted her into his arms as if she weighed nothing at all and walked her into the bedroom. His strength impressed her all over again as he lay her down on the bed and sat at her side.

"It's all right, lass," he crooned to her. "A lot has happened in a short time. It's normal to feel a little shaky. But I'm here, and we can get through anything together."

Chapter Twenty

K aleen sat up and cupped Cameron's cheek with one hand as she looked deep into his eyes. "Thank you. I'm not sure if I said that yet. I never imagined that helping Leonora would also somehow free my parents and bring them back. You've given me such a great gift."

"*You* are the gift," he countered. "*My* gift. The day I met you, the Mother of All gave me the best gift I could ever imagine. One that I will cherish for the rest of my life, and beyond."

Her heart melted a little bit. "You say the sweetest things." She reached up and kissed him.

She reclined as they kissed, and he followed her down onto the mattress. This time, their lovemaking was languid and lengthy. The urgency of their past encounters was tempered by the fact that they had accomplished those weighty goals that had been hanging over their heads. For this small space of time, they could relax and just be with each other without worry about the immediate future.

They undressed each other little by little, using long caresses and taking their time. When they were finally bare, they were also more than ready to get on with things, but Kaleen wanted to try something a little different.

She pushed him onto his back, coaxing him with kisses and gentle touches. He went willingly, seemingly ready to embrace whatever she had in mind. Then, she straddled him and reached between them, guiding him into position so she could sink down onto him.

The sensation was delicious and made her gasp as the penetration felt both different and enticing. When he was fully seated, she paused and met his gaze.

"Well, don't stop there, lass," he breathed. She could feel the tension building in his taut muscles, just as it was building in her own body.

"Just stopping to savor the moment," she told him. "Don't worry."

He smiled as his hands went to her hips. She shivered, moving a little on top of him, rotating her hips slightly to enjoy the new sensations. This was going to be epic.

She began to move, using her thighs to lift herself up and down over him. Cameron assisted, his hands gripping her hips a bit more tightly. She loved the feel of them on her skin, pressing but not hurting in any way. Just...strong and a little bit forceful in the best possible way.

She started off slow, then allowed the pressure to build slowly, using her hips to add just a hint of rotation as well as the thrusting motion that was driving her wild. At some point, she lost control and shuddered around him. That's when Cameron took over.

He turned them so that she was under him, and he raised her legs around his slim hips, sliding home again and again as she tried to reclaim her wits. He hadn't yet come, but she was well on her way to a whole new climax, and he kept driving her higher.

His pace increased, and her body reached for something just ahead. Straining together, he pushed her over the edge into oblivion a mere moment before he joined her there. He held her close, strain in every muscle of his body as he joined her in a beautiful, perfect completion.

Long after, he continued to hold her close. He'd repositioned them so that he could spoon her from behind, snuggling her into his larger, harder body. She loved the way he made her feel. She loved everything about him.

"I never really understood what a true mating was," he mused aloud, behind her, "until now."

"Funny, I was just thinking something similar," she told him, turning slightly so she could see his face. "I really do love you, Cameron."

"And I really do love you too, Kaleen."

They sealed that declaration with a kiss that led to a whole new round of pleasure that lasted well into the night.

The High Priestess arrived unexpectedly the next afternoon, surprising everyone by just suddenly appearing outside the Pack house. She knocked firmly on the front door—which was something that rarely happened at that house since very few people could reach that far into Pack territory without being noticed.

Jason, who was seated at the dining room table with the other dryad couples, shot to his feet and answered the door himself. He seemed flabbergasted to discover Bettina standing on the other side, a mischievous grin on her face. He welcomed her, and she walked through the arch into the dining room, greeting Sally first, as the Alpha female of the Pack, as shifter protocol demanded.

Bettina was a lovely woman. Petite and blonde, fair of skin, with an almost ethereal countenance. Kaleen recognized fey blood when she saw it. The High Priestess had to be pure fey. Sally and Jason introduced Bettina around to everyone. They had all lingered at the table, talking after lunch, sipping coffee, tea, or some other beverage of choice.

"I wanted to be sure to come and meet everybody before you all began dispersing to your various homes," Bettina told them. "And there was enough residual magical power in the area left from your working of the Elven Star to hide my use of a short transport hop here and back." She smiled and Kaleen made a note to ask Cameron later what the High Priestess meant because Kaleen didn't want to interrupt when Bettina was addressing everyone. "Your magical working did not go unnoticed. It has been many lifetimes since anyone even attempted an Elven Star in the mortal realm, and the way you dissipated the energy into permanent wards created ripple effects that have spread over the continent. Anybody with even a trace of magical sensitivity and know-how has figured out that something big happened here." Bettina's beautiful face held a fierce expression, then lightened. "Of course, thanks to those wards, they can't do much about it. Your territory, like Grizzly Cove, is now a no-go zone for evil and will be for many generations to come, if not forever."

"We've been testing the wards, but we never really had much experience with such things," Jason admitted. "Are they really that strong?"

Bettina nodded and smiled. "They really are among the finest examples of wards I have ever seen. They will repel anyone or anything with evil intent. Your Pack's territory is now among the few places on this planet where evil cannot go. It is a blessing from She whom I serve." Bettina winked at Jason. "You must be a really good Alpha to earn that sort of protection."

"It's not me," Jason said, humbly. "It's the entire Pack, and Leonora, and Dmitri."

Kaleen recalled the news they had received that morning that the wards extended clear down to include Dmitri and Carly's farm, which was on a lower slope of the mountain. Kaleen hadn't expected the wards would extend that far when they'd been planning to dissipate the Elven Star's energy that way, but there had been even more power generated by that spell than she'd expected, and the wards had extended farther down the mountain than they'd intended. It was just as well, though, because the Pack owned everything within the bounds of the wards except for the farm.

"And don't forget the Wraiths," Bettina added. "Their exploits and service to the Light has been noted." Bettina looked around at everyone. "It's all of you. The entire Pack and the way you've banded together to help and protect Others. As a result of your good work, your lands are now protected for all time. But this protection carries with it an obligation to continue to help Others as you have in the past, and in new ways."

"What new ways?" Sally asked, clearly a little leery of the unexpected price tag that might come of having done what they'd done.

"Have you noticed that your wards extend down the mountain to places the Pack currently doesn't use? There are even a couple of farms on the lower slopes that are included that the Pack doesn't yet own," Bettina said, a sly expression on her face.

"Yet?" Jason repeated her word. "Are we supposed to buy them?"

"I would suggest that, yes. You should definitely look into acquiring those properties that are within the wards," she replied immediately.

"And just why would we need to expand Pack lands that far? We have a big Pack now, but the land we have is more than adequate for our numbers," Sally put in, speaking slower than her usual pace and seeming to choose her words carefully.

"I will just point out that wards like the ones you now have are rarer than diamonds in this realm, and a war is coming, if it hasn't already started," Bettina said respectfully. "There may be need of such protected places as refuge for those fighting on our side in the coming battles. Places for them to recuperate, and for some of the more fragile souls to hide in safety while war rages around the world. It could be that She whom I serve has an additional role in mind for your Pack, now that you have such strong wards and such a solid and capable Alpha pair at the helm. All I ask is that you think about it...and keep an eye on those properties. If they come on the market and you can't swing the purchase yourselves, let me know, and the Lords may be able to help you."

Jason nodded noncommittally, and Bettina turned to fix her gaze on Cameron and Kaleen. "Now, as for you two," Bettina began.

Kaleen sucked in a breath. She didn't want to be in trouble with the High Priestess.

"The Lords would like to confer with you both, when you have leave to travel to their base in Montana," Bettina said, and Kaleen breathed a sigh of relief. "It's not often we have a royal wedding uniting two of the fey court's oldest and most revered noble lines."

"Wait, what?" Sally broke in to ask, looking confusedly from Kaleen to Bettina.

"Kaleen's mother is a duchess in the fey realm. And Cameron is the youngest son of the current monarch. He is actually Prince Cameron, and your cousin is properly Lady Kaleen. Of course, we're in the mortal realm and in the United States to boot, which is a place not overly concerned with noble titles."

"Nor are we," Cameron put in. "I'm very far down the line of succession, which allows me to choose the life I want, unlike the rest of my siblings. I don't expect or want the royal treatment, so please forget you heard what the High Priestess just said. After all, she did the same. Isn't that right, Aunt Bettina?"

"Hush, child," Bettina said, laughing at Cameron.

"If she's your aunt, and she did the same as you, then our High Priestess is...um...your father's younger sister?" Maria asked, trying to make sense of things.

Cameron touched his nose and pointed at Maria, nodding as he grinned.

"So, you're a princess too?" Sally asked Bettina.

"*Was*," Bettina emphasized the word. "I gave up that life to forge my own path here, and that's all I'll say on the matter." Her tone brooked no argument, and she went on. "However, there remains an issue for Kaleen and Cameron to consider." Bettina turned back to the couple. "The ring. While it will likely come in very handy in the coming battles, after they are over, and if it survives, the ring should really go back to the fey realm, where it belongs. Whether it goes with you, if you decide to live there, or it is passed on to your uncle, Kaleen, or one of his children, if he has any by then, you must consider it. I would hope that someday you can get to know your mother's younger brother. He is a good man, from all accounts, and deserves a chance at forging his own destiny now that he is out from under his uncle's tyranny. The ring would be of great help to him in that and will return stability to your ancestral lands in the fey realm."

"You still care what happens there," Maria said slowly, almost as if thinking aloud.

Bettina turned to her and nodded. "It is the realm of my birth, and as a priestess, I care for the welfare of all beings, everywhere." Bettina shrugged. "Even if I chose to make my life here, in the mortal realm."

Kaleen had to wonder why Bettina had chosen what amounted to exile here, when she clearly still cared a great deal about the fey realm and the people in it. Kaleen's own mother had forsaken the fey realm out of love for her mate, but

Bettina was unmarried as far as Kaleen knew. What could have made her give up everything she'd ever known to live here, in the much more limited mortal realm? It certainly was a mystery, but Kaleen figured she might never know the answer.

At that point, Leonora came in and greeted Bettina as an old friend. The two powerful women went off together, in search of Kaleen's parents, who had opted to take a walk directly after lunch while the younger couples had lingered at the table. That left the rest of them to take in what had just happened. The others looked merely curious, while Kaleen felt a bit shell-shocked. She wasn't used to discussing the fey realm so openly and had never had this many friends and family that she knew she could trust beyond the shadow of a doubt.

"I didn't realize the High Priestess was fey," Pam said into the silence. "I wonder what brought her here?"

"To the mortal realm?" Cameron asked, taking up the topic. "That's easy. Same thing that brought me. The need to stop Elspeth before she destroyed another realm entirely."

"Destroyed... You mean the name is more than just fearmongering?" Sally asked.

"I'm sad to say, it is. Elspeth has been around a very long time. I only became involved in the fight during her last visit to this realm. My aunt has been involved since the beginning. Elspeth's first target was the realm of her birth. The fey realm. She did her best to take over and, in the process, destroy the fabric of the realm itself as her route to what she believes is ultimate power. My father led the armies that finally defeated her, but she escaped Between and went elsewhere to begin her rampage of volatile magic all over again. She had utterly destroyed two other realms before anybody noticed. Or so I've been taught. Only the greatest mages among us can travel to the other realms. For someone like me—a simple soldier—I'm limited to fey and here. These two realms are closely aligned on the ethereal planes and do not require as much energy to navigate. Though, as you all felt when we did the spell to bring back Kaleen's parents, it does take quite a bit. Nobody travels Between lightly except for those well versed in arcane magics that are forbidden to all but the most gifted of mages."

"This is all new information to us," Jesse said shrewdly. "Why now?"

"Because the time for secrets is over. There have been signs for the past few months that Elspeth is back. The reappearance of ancient magical artifacts. The appearance of the leviathan. The fact that Admiral Morrow came out of hiding to help his sons finally defeat it. The incredible new ward you have here that is much larger and more powerful than even I expected it to be. The way my aunt has been behaving. All of it tells me that we're in for a very wild ride ahead, and unless you know everything that we know about how to fight Elspeth and her followers, you may not survive," Cameron said quietly.

"You've fought her before," Jesse went on. "We're definitely going to need your intel."

"And you shall have it," Cameron promised solemnly. "I am here, as I was the last time, to fight against Elspeth. My aunt has been following in Elspeth's tracks for eons, fighting her wherever she surfaces. Our goal is to end her for all time, but she's a slippery fish who runs when she thinks she cannot prevail and waits to try again later."

"What do you mean when you say she *destroyed* two other realms?" Maria asked, almost cringing as she spoke.

"Just that. Her chaotic magic tears at the very fabric of the world itself, while her followers wreak havoc on anyone who is not on their side. Cities destroyed. Farmland burned. Millions of beings slaughtered. All to fuel her need for chaos and death."

"Why does she do it? What is she seeking with that kind of energy?" Sally asked, shaking her head.

"Elspeth was a very gifted mage from her earliest days. She had a rather insane theory about how to achieve ultimate power. She believed she could elevate herself to godhood by conquering the energies of the ethereal plane." Cameron shrugged. "At least, that's what I've been told. I'm not enough of a mage to really understand her theories, but I've been told they are both dangerous and insane. Our goal is to stop her from destroying anything else, and stop her once and for all."

"Why do people follow her?" Pam asked in a small voice. "Surely, they realize that, if this realm is destroyed, they will be too?"

"She promises them things. Whatever each of her followers most desires. She shows the mages just enough of her *forbidden* skills to lure them in, and once she has them, they are hers. Sadly, there always seem to be people willing to make a deal with the devil in order to gain personal power." Cameron shook his head regretfully.

"That's awful," Maria said into the silence that followed Cameron's stark words.

"It is," Cameron agreed. "Which is why we really have to stop her. I'm hoping that this time will be the last time she wreaks her havoc on any realm, and we're all going to have to band together to make that happen."

"The Wraiths are with you," Jesse declared quietly.

"So is the Pack," Jason said firmly.

"The High Priestess assures me that the Lords are on board with her mission, and if they haven't already, they're going to be asking for the support of all the Tribes, Packs and Clans under their jurisdiction," Cameron put in. "We know several Masters including Dmitri and Marco who can be counted on, as can the powerful Napa Valley contingent of Marc LaTour, Atticus Maxwell, and their friends. There are other bloodletter groups around the country as well."

"And other military units," Jesse added. "Those bears in Grizzly Cove will be in on any action, you can be sure, plus the admiral has a number of special units under his command, including a top-secret base of shifters and some other talented individuals stationed just off of Long Island."

"I can try to interface with the admiral," Cameron replied, clearly thinking of his next steps in preparing for all-out war.

Kaleen didn't like the sound of any of this, but she liked the idea of the Destroyer running amok in the world of man even less.

"I'll help make that connection," Jesse volunteered at once.

The men nodded at each other, and nothing more was said on the matter. Silence descended once again.

"This is really real, huh?" Maria said finally, sounding a little scared but also resigned.

"I'm afraid so," Cameron confirmed. "Those two we defeated on the highway claimed Elspeth was already here, so we'd best get prepared and ready for anything."

The group split up after that, each going their separate ways. Some of the dryads and their mates would be leaving in a few days, heading back to their own homes. They'd extended their stay already, so the ladies could spend more time with Leonora, learning how to best use their newly enhanced powers. In fact, they spent the afternoon in the forest, with Leonora, in training.

For a few hours, Kaleen could almost forget the seriousness of their earlier discussion. She loved being out in the forest, and her father was also taking lessons on being an earth elemental, so she got to spend time with him as well. It was interesting to note the way their powers all differed slightly.

Her dad had a real way with metals in the earth while Pam was great with dirt and boulders, as well as sculpting with living trees and branches. Kaleen was the best with flowers while Crystal did amazing things with vines. Each had their own unique spin on a common ability, and Leonora seemed thrilled with it all, clapping her hands merrily when one of them showed her something new and unexpected.

They all trooped back to the Pack house for dinner to find that the men had been having a big planning session. There were maps of the area spread on the big round table in the dining room that they seemed to gravitate toward whenever they were in that room. There were also scribbled notepads by every man's elbow.

"No laptops or tablets?" Crystal asked as she went to Marco and put her arm around his waist as he returned the favor.

"We're going old school as much as possible," Jason replied. "After the bugging incident, we're not going to take as many chances as before. We're close to certain the area is clean now after all our searching, but the wards don't keep out mundane electronic devices or prevent someone from hacking our computers.

It's harder to hack good old-fashioned pen and paper, right?" He held up his pen and grinned a little.

That made sense to Kaleen as she joined Cameron at the table. Jesse started rolling up the maps, and the other men helped clear off the table. The serving tables were starting to fill, and other Pack members were already eating at other tables around the big room. It was dinnertime, and the planning could wait an hour or two while they refreshed themselves and refueled.

After dinner, the men filled the ladies in on their preliminary plans. Now that strong permanent wards encircled the Pack's territory, they were looking to expand their holdings. Jason had been busy and had already made several offers to some neighbors. Surprisingly, three had already accepted, claiming they wanted to move closer to the city now that they were older and couldn't get around as well.

Two ranchers and one woman who had inherited a tract of land that was covered by the ward were ready to sell, and Jason was moving forward as quickly as possible with the land purchases. The question was what they should do with the extra land. The High Priestess had hinted at possible uses, and one thing Jason wanted more than almost anything else was a healing facility where those who had been injured in magical battles could come for treatment of the magical variety.

That would require specialists that they didn't currently have in the Pack. Healers. True healers that used magic and could heal magical wounds. It was a specialty, and Jesse had taken the lead on putting the word out that the Pack was looking to interview a few of those kinds of people with an eye toward setting them up in one of the new properties. After all, if war was coming, healers would need a safe place to work from, perhaps more than anyone else.

The lands lower down the mountain could be used for those who could no longer fight due to injury. Or those who needed time and a safe place to heal before going back out there and engaging the enemy.

Likewise, Jason was concerned about those Others who were just too old to fight. They could easily become targets of the enemy because magical power didn't decrease with age. In fact, mostly, it increased. Killing an aged and infirm human mage and stealing their power was an easy hit for a blood path mage. Jason didn't want to see that happen.

With the new wards, they could let such people take refuge on the edges of Pack territory. If the wards let them in, they were likely on the right side of the fight. The wards wouldn't let anyone who had evil intent through, so it was a good way to screen those who asked to take up residence within the wards.

"We're going to bring in someone from Redstone Construction to see about upgrading or even building all-new facilities on the new properties, once the deals are done," Jason went on describing some of the plans they'd made that afternoon. "They're the best and the fastest, and they're mostly shifters, which counts in their favor. They know what sorts of buildings and amenities we need and can get it done quickly for a reasonable price."

"You could also offer them the use of the new facilities for their wounded or vulnerable. Agreements like that could bring down the initial cost for your Pack," Marco suggested. He was, after all, a businessman who had been in business a *lot* longer than anyone else in the room.

"A good idea, Master Marco," Jason said with respect as he made notes on the pad he'd retrieved once they'd cleared the table of their dishes.

Everybody was enjoying coffee, tea and other beverages along with dessert. The mood was mellower than it had been, but Kaleen still felt the importance of their planning. The idea of going to war was frightening, but with men like these on the right side of things, she felt better than she would otherwise.

Cameron reached for her hand. He took it and squeezed gently, as if sensing her distress.

"It will be all right," he whispered to her. "I've done battle with this enemy before and lived to tell the tale. So has Marco, and many of his brethren. We will prevail, and all this planning with make certain of it."

Kaleen realized the table around them had gone quiet. She looked around, realizing most of them were looking at her. Shifters. They could hear a pin drop a mile away, no doubt.

"He's right, you know," Jesse said quietly when she met his gaze. "Caution is good, but try not to fear. Fear doesn't help anything. We know what we're doing. We're going to prevail, even if this is the first go-round for some of us younger folk." Jesse sent a grin to Marco and then nodded at Cameron.

Kaleen realized that the leader of the Wraiths really wasn't afraid. He seemed to actually be looking forward to mixing it up with the *Venifucus*. She had to shake her head. *Men*. She would never understand them. Although, if she was telling the truth, she had enjoyed prevailing in the situations she'd been in recently. It had been scary, but it had also left her feeling triumphant.

If that's what the Wraiths got out of their missions, then she could understand why they kept fighting even after their so-called retirement from the government-sanctioned military. Maybe they were adrenaline junkies who got a thrill out of the danger, though they didn't seem like men who would take chances just for the sake of it. No, the careful planning they were doing here negated that idea. That gave her confidence. In them.

"I don't claim to understand, but I'm willing to put my faith in you all."

Smiles were her answer as the others took her words as the compliment she had intended. The group broke up as each of the couples went off together to their various pursuits. Arlo and Pam went up the mountain with Jesse and Maria. Both couples lived up in the Wraiths' section of the territory. Jason and Sally left the Pack house with the others, headed for their home, which wasn't too far distant. The other guests of the Pack—Crystal and Marco, Cece and Deke, Sunny and Den—all headed upstairs to their rooms. Kaleen's parents had already pled fatigue and gone to bed a while back.

Kaleen wasn't ready for sleep yet, and she felt a need to be outside, in the woods. She turned to Cameron.

"Would you mind if we took a walk outside?"

"Not at all," he replied immediately. "In fact, I'd prefer it. Good to clear my head and breathe some fresh air."

"Just what I was thinking." She took his hand, and they walked together out to the back deck, then down the steps and into the forest behind the Pack house.

They walked quietly, heading into the deeper part of the woods. It was a moment before Kaleen realized she'd been heading for the area of the willow—Leonora's willow. She stopped before it and noted the slight glow about the tree. It had been the epicenter of the magic they had wrought, and she suspected it would never be the same.

"I think this tree is now the heart of the entire grove, if it wasn't already," Kaleen said quietly, almost reverently.

"How big is the grove?" Cameron asked in a similar tone.

"I think..." She looked around, turning in a circle and closing her eyes as her hands extended a little way from her sides. When she stopped, her eyes snapped open in wonder as she looked at Cameron. "I think it's the whole mountain. This one tree is so much more powerful...more *alive*...than any other tree in the vicinity. It will watch over them all for as far as its power extends, and being inside such strong wards only helps the situation. I think the forest here will be happy for centuries to come, if not forever, with such a patient and caring guardian."

Kaleen reached out to touch a leaf just above her head and smiled. This tree was like a new friend to her, its thoughts and feelings—yes, feelings—so very close to the surface now, after all it had been through and helped happen. They all owed this tree a great debt for taking such good care of Leonora for so long. A sudden thought occurred to her.

"Where will we live?" she asked Cameron.

"Wherever you like," he replied immediately.

"Do you think my parents' house will be safe anytime soon? Not for us, but for them," she hastened to add.

"I'm not sure. They've both been through a lot and should probably get their sea legs under them again before they venture out into the wider world. They have the hospitality of the Pack for now. Maybe they can be of help in setting up the new properties lower down on the mountain or something."

"But what about their house?"

"We can probably arrange things so that someone local can look after the property. You have a lawn service, right?"

She nodded. "I have a yearly contract with a company that cuts the grass and trims the hedges. They'll tidy the flower beds if I ask them to, but I did most of that myself because I enjoyed it."

"Well, then. A few phone calls and we can have the outside taken care of by your garden crew. Then, there are probably a few shifter groups in the vicinity that we can ask to swing by the property every once in a while to make sure the place hasn't been invaded or anything like that. Most shifter Packs and Clans do have at least a few qualified people in the trades who can keep the property up to snuff. Electricians, plumbers, carpenters and the like. We can ask Jason or Jesse if they know anybody in the area that can help us out."

Kaleen nodded slowly. "If my folks decide to stay here, do you think..." She paused and tried again, suddenly nervous for some reason she couldn't decipher. "Do you think we can stay too?"

Cameron walked up to her and placed his hands on her shoulders. "You only just got them back. It's natural you want to stay near them, and there is much Leonora can teach both you and your father. I have no special need to be anywhere in particular, and, in fact, Bettina would probably like it if I stuck around and helped with the new lands the Pack is obtaining. If it's all right with the Alpha, then it's all right with me. I go wherever you go, Kaleen. You're my mate, even if we aren't shifters to know each other by scent or whatever means they use. I know deep in my heart that you were meant for me and vice versa. I don't ever want to be apart from you again, if we can possibly manage it."

Kaleen felt the tension leave her body. "We'll manage it. Somehow." She moved into his embrace and hugged him close. "Thank you for understanding about my parents. I've missed them so much. Having you in my life is a true blessing, but I don't want to leave them now that I've just found them. In time, I'm sure, we can go off and do our own thing. Whatever that may be. But for now, I'd just like to be wherever they are, if that's okay."

"It's more than okay," Cameron assured her. "It's perfectly understandable and reasonable. And, I think, they want to be around you too. They missed a lot of your life, and I think they'll want to be part of it from now on. We'll talk to them tomorrow about their plans and then talk to Jason, if it goes the way I think it'll go. Then, we'll make some phone calls to have their house taken care of in their absence, and we can probably even get some shifters to pack a few things for you and send them here or wherever we end up. Same for your parents. They probably want some of their own clothes and possessions."

"That sounds perfect," she told him, looking up into his eyes.

"If we stay here," he said slowly, as if thinking aloud, "do you want to help out with the new properties farther down the mountain? The Pack has a lot of members, but there's also a lot of new land coming to them within the wards, and probably more to come as Jason starts talking to the other remaining landowners. I suspect they could use our help."

"I'd enjoy that," Kaleen replied, already warming to the idea.

They could be near enough to her family to spend a lot of time together, yet probably still have their own place. It was a great solution, especially since they'd be helping the Pack and whoever else was going to need sanctuary here after the war they were all expecting got started in earnest. She liked the idea of helping prepare. It would be wrong to just sit around as the threat approached, especially now that she understood more about what was coming for them all.

"We'll talk to your folks first, then see where we go from there, but I like this plan," Cameron looked down into her eyes, satisfaction and his adventurous spirit shining in his.

"I like it too," she replied, feeing saucy, "but I *love* you."

He growled in response and lowered his lips to hers. "I love you too, little sparrow. My One. My only," he whispered just before sealing his declaration with a tempestuous kiss.

As the world faded around them and they focused solely on each other, the wildwood rejoiced. The dryads had come home, and there were more of them in this realm than had been seen in eons. In due course, every forest in the world would feel their power, and the woodlands felt the promise of renewal.

Further, they had all found their perfect mates, which meant they might all be creating new little dryad-touched lives in the future. Their lines would perpetuate, and the earth would be renewed in their wake. There might be trouble ahead for the inhabitants of this realm, but the earth itself should endure. Having the dryads here in force meant that the earth would have seven new champions when the Destroyer came again.

As far as the earth was concerned, things were definitely looking up.

Bonus Epilogue

Wyoming Pack Territory

While all the dryads and their mates went upstairs to seek their beds in the Pack house after helping Kaleen and Cameron go Between to retrieve Kaleen's parents from the fey realm, Leonora held Marco and Crystal back. She asked them to follow her outside onto the back deck and they complied. She could tell they were curious but willing to humor her. Once they were outside, she turned to them.

"I want you both to know of the bargain that I made with Master Dmitri. It wasn't a formal agreement in any way, but his willingness to help sustain my life while I was so grievously injured, and his friendship throughout the many years, including his vigilance in guarding my resting place while Sally gathered everybody together, have decided me on a course of action that some would consider radical."

Leonora knew they had heard of the way Dmitri had given a few drops of his immortal blood to help sustain her while she rested in the willow tree. Without his contribution, she probably would be dead by now. She owed him. Not just for that, but for the many years he had stood by her. They had been neighbors for a very long time. He had made his home on the farm—or, rather, under the farm—that was relatively nearby, while she had lived in these woods for centuries. Their paths had crossed many times and she counted him among her friends. One of the few friends who might live as long as she would.

She had watched him these many years. She thought she knew his character, and since he had found his mate, she had seen him transform into a joyful person. For such as he, there was only one true mate who could complete them, and Leonora had rejoiced when she learned that Dmitri had found his. She counted them both as friends now and wanted to see them happy.

"I think I know what you're going to say, milady," Marco said respectfully, "and based on my own recent experience, and what I know of Dmitri and his mate, and the trouble that is sure to come to the mortal realm sooner than we all wish, I think it is a good decision on your part. The more powerful fighters we have on the side of Light, the better, and Dmitri has always been a fierce warrior and a man of honor."

"You do know that he had to turn his mate in order to save her life, don't you? What I propose to do, will affect them both," Leonora reminded him.

Marco shrugged. "They are mates. She is the other half of his soul. She could no more be evil, then he could. I have no fear of the power you will give them both." He chuckled a little. "To be honest, the power is secondary to the freedom. Until Crystal accepted me as her mate, I had not walked in the sun since I was a young man in Italy in the Middle Ages. Her blood—her magic—made me a daywalker, and if that is what you propose to do to Dmitri and his mate, I have no objection from the bloodletter standpoint."

"You mean, you're going to give Dmitri some of your blood, and it will allow him to be in the sun without going up in flames?" Crystal asked. Leonora reminded herself that Crystal was new to all of this. She hadn't known much about magic until she met Marco.

"Precisely, my dear. He gave me his blood. I propose to give him some of mine, in return." She tilted her head and thought about it for a moment. "It will change him. Permanently. The magic will blend and merge and make him more powerful than he was before. Which, for someone as old as he is, is quite powerful enough already. But his mate is young in years and experience. As she feeds from him, remnants of my power will pass to her, as well. It is something to be considered. But, as Marco rightly points out, since Dmitri's honor is beyond question, so too, should his mate's be. He could not find the other half to his soul in someone with even a shred of evil in theirs." Leonora shook out her arms and shrugged. "Good. That's settled. I wanted to make sure you knew, so that perhaps the four of you could discuss this before you go back home. Perhaps your experiences could help them prepare for the changes that are about to happen in their lives."

Marco bowed his head in respect, holding her gaze. "Yes, milady. It would be my honor. And, as you probably realize, the secret of being a daywalker must be kept, I believe, until such time as our enemy makes their move. If they think I can only be effective at night, they will get a very large surprise if they come at me by day."

"Do as you think best, of course, Master Marco. I believe you are correct in holding your secret, and I will abide by whatever you and Dmitri decide. Nobody will hear of your new abilities from me." She smiled at him. "Oh, and you should probably think about how the changes in Crystal's abilities will affect you. She took quite a jump in magical power last night. I suspect, over time, that will affect you, as well."

Marco cocked his head and one dark eyebrow rose. "I had not considered that, I confess. Thank you for the warning, milady. I will be on the watch for fluctuations in our power levels. I expect, this will all take some getting used to."

Leonora laughed. "I suspect you're right, but so far, it's all to the good for our side."

Leonora didn't waste time but called Dmitri a short while later. He wasn't far. He had been teaching his beloved how to fly, and they both came to meet Leonora in the woods just outside the Pack house shortly after she called.

Leonora had met Carly a number of times, already. She was a lovely young woman with a great deal of technical skill in the field of computer programming. That's how she and Dmitri had met, apparently. When Carly's small business had been hired to do some upgrades to the computer network at the college where Dmitri taught night classes, they had met and he had known almost instantly that she was his destined mate.

To further that idea, she had not so coincidentally purchased the farmhouse that lay just above Dimitri's underground lair. He had built his subterranean home centuries ago and formed an alliance with the farmer who lived above. Subsequent generations of that family had always been in on the deal. They protected Dimitri's home by day, and they profited greatly from his protection at night, and his business acumen.

The arrangement had worked very well for Dimitri and the people who had agreed to help him for many, many years, but the last living descendent of that line had died and the farm had been sold. To Carly, as it turned out. She'd been a city girl looking for a change of pace. Her work had burned her out mentally and physically and she had wanted to find a place in the country to relax and get away from the demands of her business.

What she hadn't expected, was to find an ancient vampire living beneath her new farmhouse. Even more unexpectedly, he had turned out to be her mate. And, when she'd come as close to death as possible without crossing over, she had decided to choose the night—and Dmitri—over death. He had changed her, and brought her back to his lair, as his bride.

They had been deliriously happy ever since. Carly had gone to college with Sally, and when Sally had come to visit, she had met Jason. More fated mates and happy marriages. Leonora was a strong believer that the Mother of All played a much bigger role in everyone's lives than they believed.

"Thank you for coming," Leonora greeted Dimitri and Carly as she took a seat on a fallen tree trunk. There might be a few wolves prowling around the area, but Dimitri was an old ally of the Pack, and his mate was best friends with the Alpha female. Nobody would object to either one of them being in Pack territory.

"It is my pleasure to see you in the mortal realm once again, my friend," Dimitri said.

"I'm glad to be here," Leonora said honestly. "And I must thank you for all that you have done to make this possible. I owe you a great deal."

Dmitri held up his hands, palms outward and looked down. "You owe me nothing, my friend. I mean that. What I did, I did out of friendship and the desire to see your life continue. Nothing more. I mean that."

"I know you do," Leonora replied immediately, smiling fondly at him. "However, there is something I can do for you that I think is important. It will affect you, quite possibly permanently, and it will also affect your mate, so I wanted to give you an opportunity to think it through. As it happens, one of my granddaughters mated one of your kind recently. You know Master Marco, of course." Dmitri nodded in acknowledgment. "His abilities have...changed. He can now walk in the sun."

Dimitri's expression changed to one filled with wonder and disbelief. "How can this be?"

"The mixture of dryad magic with bloodletter magic creates something different." Leonora shrugged.

"A daywalker?" Once again, disbelief colored Dimitri's tone.

"What's a daywalker?" Carly asked.

Dimitri looked at his mate. "A bloodletter, with all of our powers, who need not fear the sun. It's a myth. Something talked about in whispers, but never seen."

"Until now," Leonora said with authority. "I can assure you, Marco is now a daywalker, thanks to the blood of his mate, my many-times-great-granddaughter. I propose to repay the blood you gave me to sustain my life, with a bit of my blood for you, to change your life—and quite possibly your mate's life—for the better."

Dmitri looked from Leonora to Carly. His gaze took on a look of love and hope when he regarded his mate.

"You could walk in the sun again, without fear," he told her.

Carly took his hand in hers and looked deep into his eyes. "You know I don't need the sun as long as I have you. Don't do this unless it's what *you* want."

"I want you to know that I already talked to Marco and Crystal about this. They have agreed to talk this over with you both if you like, since they have been dealing with these issues recently. One thing Marco did say that you should take into account is that they are keeping his new abilities as secret as possible. Holding it in reserve against any enemy who might come at them during the day, assuming Marco would be weakened by the sun. It can be an ace in the hole, as they say. I might also add that we all expect that if the Destroyer isn't back in this realm already, she will be soon. Her followers grow bolder every day and have targeted those of us on the side of Light. This change might give you an edge that could help protect you both, should you come under attack again."

Dmitri regarded her with a frown. "These are all good points, milady, and your offer is incredibly generous."

"No more generous than you were when I was in need. I will never forget your kindness and willingness to help me when I was so close to leaving this realm permanently. You saved my life, Dmitri. I will never forget that." Leonora spoke the words like a vow and saw that he understood. "I do not make this offer lightly, nor would I make it to anyone else. Only you have earned this through your purity of heart, strength of mind and the purity of your honor." She shook her head and smiled. "We've been friends a long time. You're not the only bloodletter I know, but you're the only one I would trust with this sort of power. Especially after the events of the past few years. I want to do what I can to make sure that when the time comes and you are fighting the forces of evil once more, you have every weapon available to you to save yourself and your mate and rid this realm of the evil that came after you."

Dmitri held her gaze for a moment longer, then bowed deeply. "I am your humble servant, milady."

He still had those old-world manners that made her smile. Leonora looked at Carly and beckoned her to sit beside her. "I'm going to give the blood to him," Leonora told Carly. "I think you're still too young in your power to be able to handle this sort of thing, but you will get the effect from him, the next time you take his blood," Leonora explained. "As it is, he's probably going to be a little...um...odd, for a bit. I can't really predict what my magic will do to him right off the bat. I suspect he'll have a power surge at first and then he's going to have to get used to the way the magics merge and settle into a new configuration within him. I want you to watch over him. Take him home right after this and see to it that he rests for a good long while. Don't drink from him until he is stable. It wouldn't do to have you both acting weird and unsettled at the same time. Understood?"

Carly looked worried but nodded.

"All right." Leonora turned back to Dmitri. "You, my old friend, come here." She patted the tree trunk on her other side.

Dmitri came to her and sat down. Leonora offered him her wrist, then pulled it back and met his gaze.

"Don't take too much. You only need a couple of drops for the effect to take hold. If you take more, it will be too strong to handle at first. A small amount is better for this kind of thing. The power gain should be more gradual, and you'll have time to get home and settle in before the real changes start to occur."

"Yes, milady. I understand. I—" He paused, then tried again. "I can't believe this is actually happening. That you would do this for me, and my mate."

"It is happening, and you have earned this, my friend. Let's hear no more of it." She offered him her wrist again, and he took it gingerly.

As Leonora steeled herself for his bite, he met her gaze. He smiled at her.

"I assure you. This will not hurt. It's one of the first things we learn. How to make it painless for the donor," he told her with kindness. "I think it's even nicer of you to volunteer, considering it's obvious you thought this would bring you pain."

"Stop talking, and get on with it," Leonora groused with good humor. It was clear he was dragging this out because he knew as well as she did, that this would change everything for him and his mate.

"As you wish, milady." He raised her wrist to his mouth and kissed her skin.

She could feel his tongue peep out to lick the skin over her vein, anesthetizing the area. A moment later and he released her hand. She examined her wrist carefully but couldn't see any bite marks.

"Did you do it?" She looked up at him and was amazed to see the power roiling in his eyes. "Ah, yes. I can see that you have. Good." She stood up and motioned to Carly. "Time for you to take him home. See that he gets a good rest and remember not to bite him again until his power has settled."

"Leonora!" Dimitri's voice was hoarse, his eyes still roiling with unsettled power. "This is amazing," he whispered. "Thank you. Thank you from the bottom of my heart."

Carly took his hand and led him a few steps away. Leonora watched them go and admired the bond between them. It was so obvious to see. They were very much in love and well matched.

"Thank you, my friend. Be happy. Both of you."

Carly and Demetri took to the air in a fine mist and disappeared. Just one of the amazing abilities the ancient bloodletters developed over their years. Carly was very talented, indeed, to have learned to do that in such a short time. Leonora was confident that Carley would watch over her mate until the magic settled. She looked forward to seeing them both again—perhaps in the sunshine—and was glad she had been able to give him such a gift. There were very few she would trust with such power.

Leonora walked back to the house alone. She tried not to think about how long it had been since her love affair with the woodcutter and the birth of her one and only daughter, Marisol. The centuries had blended together after his death, and she had let time pass without realizing it. Now, things had changed for her. She was surrounded by descendants and had more family than she had ever had before. But still, she was lonely.

They were all mated, and so happy. She didn't begrudge them a moment of their happiness, but she started to realize what she had been missing all these many years. She wasn't sure how it would happen, but perhaps there would be a time for her to find love again.

Dryads weren't like bloodletters. They didn't spend centuries searching for their One. Elemental powers could, and did, find mates among the other races, but not as easily or as quickly as Others. Now that she was back, and healthy, Leonora thought she might visit the only other elemental she knew.

Admiral Morrow, as he was now known, had found his mate in a mortal woman who'd already had a son by her first husband. That son, Deke, was now mated to one of Leonora's granddaughters. So, in essence, Leonora was now family. An earth elemental related to a water elemental. Would wonders never cease?

She chuckled to herself as she went back into the house. She would like to speak to Don Morrow, as he was calling himself these days. She'd known him centuries before when he'd been going by a single name. A famous name. Back then, people had called him Poseidon and he'd been lapping it up, masquerading as a god.

He'd been full of himself, and Leonora had enjoyed playing tricks on him. They'd been like rival siblings, way back then. Maybe he could give her some advice on how to proceed in the modern world. He seemed to have matured and found his way to contribute. Maybe he could give her some pointers.

That plan firmly in mind, Leonora made her way to the guestroom and finally went to bed.

About the Author

Bianca D'Arc has run a laboratory, climbed the corporate ladder in the shark-infested streets of lower Manhattan, studied and taught martial arts, and earned the right to put a whole bunch of letters after her name, but she's always enjoyed writing more than any of her other pursuits. She grew up and still lives on Long Island, where she keeps busy with an extensive garden, several aquariums full of very demanding fish, and writing her favorite genres of paranormal, fantasy and sci-fi romance.

Bianca loves to hear from readers and can be reached through Facebook (BiancaDArcAuthor) or through the various links on her website.

Welcome to The D'Arc Side...

WWW.BIANCADARC.COM

Also By Bianca D'Arc

Simon Says
Once Bitten
Smoke on the Water
Night Shade
Shadow Play

Epic Fantasy Erotic Romance

Dragon Knights ~ Daughters of the Dragon
Maiden Flight*
Border Lair
The Ice Dragon**
Prince of Spies***

Dragon Knights ~ The Novellas
The Dragon Healer
Master at Arms
Wings of Change

Dragon Knights ~ Sons of Draconia
FireDrake
Dragon Storm
Keeper of the Flame
Hidden Dragons

Dragon Knights ~ The Sea Captain's Daughter Trilogy
Sea Dragon
Dragon Fire
Dragon Mates

Dragon Knights ~ Rise of the Jinn
The Captain's Dragon
Snow Dragon
Gatekeeper
Spymaster

Science Fiction Romance

StarLords
Hidden Talent

Talent For Trouble

Shy Talent

Jit'Suku Chronicles ~ In the Stars
The Cyborg Next Door

Heart of the Machine

Jit'Suku Chronicles ~ Arcana
King of Swords

King of Cups

King of Clubs

King of Stars

End of the Line

Diva

Jit'Suku Chronicles ~ Sons of Amber
Angel in the Badlands

Master of Her Heart

Starcrossed

Futuristic Erotic Romance

Resonance Mates
Hara's Legacy**

Davin's Quest

Jaci's Experiment

Grady's Awakening

Harry's Sacrifice

Contemporary Romance

Irish Lullaby
Bells Will Be Ringing
Wild Irish Rose

* RT Book Reviews Awards Nominee

** EPPIE Award Winner

*** CAPA Award Winner

Made in the USA
Monee, IL
13 August 2023

40943446R00105